SHE'S ALWAYS HUNGRY

Also by Eliza Clark

PENANCE

BOY PARTS

She's Always Hungry

Stories

ELIZA CLARK

HARPER PERENNIAL

NEW YORK • LONDON • TORONTO • SYDNEY • NEW DELHI • AUCKLAND

HARPER PERENNIAL

Originally published in the United Kingdom in 2024 by Faber & Faber Limited.

HarperCollins books may be purchased for educational, business, or sales promotional use. For information, please email the Special Markets Department at SPsales@harpercollins.com.

FIRST U.S. EDITION

Library of Congress Cataloging-in-Publication Data

Names: Clark, Eliza, 1994- author.
Title: She's always hungry : stories / Eliza Clark.
Description: First HarperPerennial edition. | New York, NY : Harper Perennial, 2024.
Identifiers: LCCN 2024025657 | ISBN 9780063393264 (trade paperback) | ISBN
  9780063393271 (ebook)
Subjects: LCGFT: Short stories.
Classification: LCC PS3603.H357276 S54 2024 | DDC 813/.6--dc23/
eng/20240614
LC record available at https://lccn.loc.gov/2024025657

ISBN 978-0-06-339326-4 (pbk.)

24 25 26 27 28 LBC 5 4 3 2 1

Content note: This collection contains themes and subject matter some readers may find disturbing.

If you would like more information before proceeding, please check the detailed content guide on page 221 ahead of reading.

Contents

SHE'S ALWAYS HUNGRY

Build a Body Like Mine

It doesn't have to look like mine; I mean a body that *works* like mine. You can look however you want. Is your perfect body, *hard*? Is it soft in the *right places*? Is it hollow? Picture it. Picture your perfect self. Touch your stomach. Imagine it free of excess – imagine you at your tightest; your body constrained and efficient.

All while eating *whatever you want.*

That's right. Whatever you want. No fine print, no asterisk, no vomiting. Whether your vice is carbs, sweets or fast food, I can get you there.

How much? you ask. You'd be surprised.

Follow a few simple steps and you can eat whatever you want (as much *and* as often as you like) *and* you'll actually lose weight. I even offer a convenient subscription service – for the woman on the go.

Find me in darker corners of the clearnet (that's right! You don't even need Tor). I'm not difficult to locate for those with determination. And what I have to offer *really* works. Find me deliciously thin at a Michelin star restaurant, devouring a tasting menu with a wasp waist, never loosening my belt. Join me at the table. Ditch your dry, miserable salads. Leave your fad diets in the dust. Restrict no more and thrive, my love.

I USED TO BE LIKE YOU.

I used to fantasise about fries from McDonald's. Salty and hot; crunchy on the outside, soft on the inside. Hard not to snap. I used to feel so guilty – but I no longer consider self-control a virtue.

What would snapping look like? Two cartons of fries sliding down my throat, followed by the burger. The salty beef, processed till it's pillow soft like the buns it's sandwiched in between. Bite it, feel the rubbery pickle squeak against my teeth, taste the onions marinated in American mustard and globs of ketchup. When I was a child, I would dismantle the burger with my tiny fingers – rip up the patty and the buns into nugget-sized pieces and dip each precious piece into a little pot of ketchup. As an adult, I'd jam my fingers down my throat, still tasting of oil and salt, those once treasured chunks of food splashing into the toilet.

And God, there's just no need to live your life like that in pursuit of a beautiful body. Not any more – not with my methods.

And I've tried a lot of methods. When I was a teenager I went to Slimming World, where they tell you food is *sinful*. Heavy women in their sixties told me I was right to start watching my weight now. They gave me a pink certificate when I lost half a stone.

When I went to university I abandoned the doctrine of Slimming World and lived in monastic starvation. I spent three years living on instant ramen, satsumas and cereal bars – with the occasional binge and purge to break the monotony. With that cocktail of restriction and my nineteen-year-old metabolism the weight fell off me and stayed off, for a time.

I looked in the mirror a lot during this time. The body I once recognised as my own had melted away. Who was this creature beneath the fat? At the time, I failed to recognise her as my best self. I thought she was nothing like a real girl. I thought she looked like something a pervert imagined; something a twelve-year-old boy doodled in the back of a notebook. A cartoon with torpedo breasts glued on to her weird, bony frame. Not a person's body, but a wasp's. A thorax, not a torso. I was wrong not to see the perfection in this form. I was wrong to treat this body as if it were not my own.

I had to buy new clothes. All of my old things were baggy. I had to drop two dress sizes to find a comfortable fit, and I felt overly optimistic buying them. I took my tiny skirts and dresses and jeans to the till and the cashier did not raise an eyebrow. I had almost expected her to laugh at me.

I threw most of my clothes from this era away; I could no longer stand the sight of them when I began to eat again.

Because I did begin to eat again.

WITH MY METHOD, YOU WILL NOT REQUIRE WILLPOWER.

Because willpower only lasts so long, I broke. I blame my partner. I think if I'd ended up with a man, I might've gotten away with it for a bit longer. Might've even gotten him to go along with it for a bit. *I'm intermittent fasting*, I'd say, or some other shit – and he probably wouldn't bat an eyelid.

But Shadi had overcome her own issues with food – something that did make me roll my eyes a little when she talked about it. She was willowy. Nothing stuck to her the way it stuck to me. It was hard not to resent her when she was so difficult to fool.

At first, I ate because we went on dates together. Because she cooked for me. Because I was happy. A happy brain resists deprivation. I denied myself when she was not there. But then she was *always* there. All-knowing, all-watching, a great big pair of black eyes, damp with concern.

When we moved in together, I ate even more. I went through phases of bingeing and purging. I tried to keep it secret, but I couldn't. She'd work it out. Vomit residue in the toilet, the smell in the bathroom or toothpaste on my breath. I didn't have the stamina for bulimia or the will for anorexia. Though she was always kind and patient; I could not take the shame when Shadi caught me. I was content with everything but my body. No depression to stave off my anxious eating. Someone to feed me. Someone to care. Someone to *nag*.

And my waist dissolved over the course of two years, gradual but sudden. I woke up one day and found that even the biggest of my little clothes no longer contained my completely average body. Stretch-marked, but not yet sagging, I was spackled with cellulite, and I jiggled and bounced with every step.

I began to miss the insect inside of me I had once found so alien to behold. I looked at happy fat women with nothing but envy. I thought about how wonderful life must be when one embraces oneself. I still think they are beautiful. Contrary to your expectations, my methods are not for them. Not for anyone who looks in the mirror and feels pleased or even neutral. I deal in sickness. My methods are a balm for the diseased, the unsatisfied, the covetous.

If you try to eat *mindfully*, to think *positively*, to covet a healthy, happy body the way you covet a thin one – you are the type of person who needs me.

HERE'S HOW I DISCOVERED MY WINNING WEIGHTLOSS TECHNIQUE.

Entirely by accident, if you can believe it!

It was Shadi who noticed it first. She put her hands upon my waist and said: *Have you lost weight?* She was trying her best to sound neutral, not to let concern prick her voice.

No, I told her.

Are you sure? she asked. And at the time, I genuinely had not noticed. I was terrified of the scale – I wore loose clothing that could not police a waistline.

But when I stepped onto the scale that night (dusty – covered in hair and splashes of dry toothpaste), lo and behold my weight had dropped about thirteen pounds. Not drastic on my frame but a *lot*.

I had been secretly restricting. Just a little. Celery for lunch. Boiled egg. Complaining of being full after eating half of one of Shadi's generous portions.

I was delighted. Shadi peered over my shoulder with her brows furrowed. She asked me if I'd been skipping lunch at work. I told her no and she didn't believe me. She told me she loved me.

That number kept tipping down. I thought my cucumber slices and dry, baked aubergines were having miraculous effects. I had fantastical, borderline erotic visions of KFC and burritos and bacon sandwiches. I smelt salt and grease, my mouth filled at the thought of special blends of spices and crispy skins; of secret sauces and baby-soft pork. I would zone out in meetings thinking of gooey, spongy Pizza Hut pizza, of dipping the crusts in hot sauce and garlic dip and straight mayonnaise (like an animal).

I watched these disgusting videos on my phone of people making 'lasagne cakes' and 'lasagne in a mug' and 'lasagne burritos' and 'lasagne nuggets'. Lasagne being twisted and reshaped into vile shadows of its former self became a form of pornography for me.

I broke four weeks into that miserable little diet. I got a McDonald's on my lunch break. I ate it furtively in a corner of the restaurant. I did not stick my fingers down my throat, but I stood over the toilet and thought about it. I cried into my pillow, and made a salad for dinner. When Shadi tried to question the salad, I barked at her. Asked her if she, from her privileged position of unearned thinness, enjoyed policing my diet.

I'm not policing, she said. *I'm worried about you.*

You're putting me on edge, I told her. *You monitoring my meals is triggering for me.* And she made a face like she didn't quite believe me.

The next day I had a burrito for lunch. The next day I ate unfranchised fried chicken, and stood in the office bathroom and beat my fists into my growling, grumbling stomach. I called myself a failure for my lack of willpower. Little did I know, I had surpassed the need for willpower. I thought I had collapsed into shameful bingeing – little did I know, I had simply ascended to a new state of being.

I got on the scale. My weight was down *again*. Another big chunk. And at that time I worried. I came to Shadi crying. I told her that I did not know what was causing the weight loss. I showed her my bank statements as proof – I had been eating lunch. I'd been eating *a lot* of lunch. This frightened her. She did not understand. At the time, neither did I. We booked me a doctor's appointment.

By the time I went, I had lost even more weight.

I worried it was a chronic health issue – something with my thyroid or my gut. Maybe cancer. A girl I went to sixth form with had cancer. She was so tiny when she came back to school and she hated being complimented for it. She would scold people who remarked, impressed, on how petite she was, how lovely she was. *I nearly died*, she'd hiss. I was so jealous of her. I was jealous of her cancer in the way only a teenager can be.

I am too old for that now. Almost dying at a young, tragic age loses its seductive qualities the moment you turn twenty-five.

THE GP WAS STUMPED . . . THEY SENT ME FOR TESTS AT THE HOSPITAL . . .

In the weeks building up to my hospital appointment, I became so thin that none of my clothes fit me properly. I rotated a few loose dresses that would not fall off my bony shoulders, hoping my friends and colleagues would not notice my dramatic weight loss. But they did. So much volume gone around my face. *What's your secret?* they cooed. At the time I had no idea; terror-stricken I said: *I don't know, I'm going to the hospital.* And they cooed, sympathetic, unable to cover their jealousy.

They were right to be jealous.

A hospital specialist found the secret in my belly.

For months, I had been incubating a parasite. There had

been a worm eating my dinners. Nesting inside me, snaking its way through my guts and huge; monstrously huge.

The specialist was horrified. *What did you eat? Where in the world have you been?*

Celery. Nowhere. I went to Sheffield for work three months ago.

He fed me a pill. I aborted my fat, flat baby. And though I had fed her and sheltered her like my own child, Shadi would not let me keep her in a jar.

MY SECRET REVEALED!

Shadi told me I looked unwell. Gaunt. *Older*, she said.

I looked great. (I STILL LOOK GREAT. My cheekbones, my jawline, my *waist*. I am a perfect pointy hourglass. Torpedo tits and xylophone ribs, I am a mother of worms; I am a cartoon girl wrought in human skin and bone.) I sighed, and told her I'd put the weight back on. Anxiety about my weight had melted away. Perhaps the worm had eaten it.

When Shadi took me for lunch, I happily ate three-fourths of a cheeseboard. I deepthroated breadsticks and bit a mozzarella ball like an apple. Manchego and honey, blue cheese and soft bread; I sucked cheese crumbs from underneath my nails. I ordered a lasagne and ate the whole thing, while Shadi looked on, pleased but concerned. Was this a binge? Or had the worm made me hungry?

I bought a slice of pizza on the way home.

AFTER WEEKS OF EATING GLORIOUSLY . . . I PUT ONLY A LITTLE WEIGHT BACK ON . . .

I had to go back to the doctor and back to the hospital again. Another worm. ANOTHER WORM! It had spontaneously appeared in my stomach – no raw meat or trips to countries with poor water sanitation. A fluke or an immaculate conception. Another worm.

Shadi googled around and came to the conclusion I had bought the second tapeworm from the dark web or something. She was angry (*Not angry! I'm frustrated and disappointed and worried!* she said.) enough with me, that I decided not to tell her if it happened again. I'd convince her my weight had merely stabilised at a point *much* lower than it had been.

Your long-term health . . . she lamented. *Weren't we talking about a baby some day?* she asked, as if I were not already a mother.

I did not go back to the doctor when I felt the third one growing inside me. I bought the stuff to evacuate it online. You can DIY most things, nowadays.

In those days, I would always evacuate the worm after a couple of months. I was worried, back then, that they would kill me. I continued to eat like a queen. Shadi was wild with concern. She lectured and cried and begged me to stop whatever it was I was doing. All because I was EATING WHAT I WANTED, AND NEVER PUTTING ON WEIGHT.

I think she was jealous. Of my body. Of my worms. She wouldn't let me go to the bathroom alone; she obsessively checked the rim of the toilet bowl for evidence of vomit. Even my toilet time was monitored. I could not take a shit in peace.

She did not believe in my new metabolism. She did not accept that my body was simply reacting and adapting to its infestation. And I swore neither my fingers nor my toothbrush had been near the back of my throat.

I find the way you're monitoring me really upsetting, I told her through tears. *You're being really controlling, Shadi. It's scary.*

She let up her close surveillance after that, but we were never the same. Didn't last much longer after that.

WHERE DO THE WORMS COME FROM? CAN I GET MY OWN?

Good question! You catch them from eating shit and raw meat, neither of which have passed my lips. I sought answers on a pro-ana forum, which I could use without shame now Shadi was gone. I asked them: *Has anyone had any experience with tapeworms?* I do not know what I expected them to tell me.

A couple of people say that they have thought about getting tapeworms; some even say that they've looked for eggs on the darknet. I recommend it. I share my experiences. An orthorexic vegan tries to pick a fight with me; *It's cruel*, she says. But it's not cruel. It's symbiotic.

But the other girls want eggs of their own. And I would soon be able to assist them.

I chose not to purge the worm inside me at that moment. Let it fester, waited, waited, waited till my period came around and I did not bleed.

I found, instead, clinging to a sanitary pad, a clutch of eggs. Like puffed rice covered in the soft skin of an egg white.

YOU GUESSED IT! I AM SELLING THEM! THAT'S RIGHT! FOR A VERY REASONABLE PRICE YOU CAN LIVE AS I DO.

I even offer a convenient subscription service – *for the woman on the go.*

I no longer purge my worms FOR I AM MORE WORM THAN WOMAN. But you must. Follow my instructions. Give in to the cycle. Incubate, purge and incubate again. Value the relationship with your worm; treat it like a foetus. Love it. Use discount code LoveIt at checkout for twenty per cent off your second order. Become your best self.

The Problem Solver

Juliet decides to tell Oscar about Friday night. She will tell him because she has to tell someone. He's a close friend, but not her first choice.

Juliet says, 'I have to talk to you about something, something serious,' and Oscar winces like Juliet is about to tell him she wants to move out. Juliet glances at the closed door to Hannah's empty room – the sting of her *big Australian move* still fresh in both of their minds. Hannah would've been Juliet's first choice to tell.

'Hang on, let me brace myself,' Oscar says, heading to the kitchen to uncork a bottle of wine and pour them each a glass before Juliet begins.

She's not moving out. Oscar is relieved, until he isn't.

The wine in his glass quivers. He is furious. He does not look at her. To his credit, he listens closely to her and he does not try to touch her. He does not interrupt. Even when she tells Oscar the name of her attacker – a casual acquaintance of theirs – he behaves. When she finishes her story she is shivering and in tears, and he hands her a tissue from a warm packet stuffed into his pocket. But he is furious – his face red with it.

'I'm so sorry,' he says. 'I'm so angry. I'm so angry that men are like this,' he adds, indignant.

'It's okay,' says Juliet.

'It's not okay. Fucking hell, Juliet, it's not okay. Have you reported it?' Juliet says no. Juliet knows she'll have to hand her phone over to the police and thinks about the unsubtle texts from her weed dealer, the photos of herself in lingerie and the four-year-old account on the website she had once used to flog her dirty underwear.

Juliet wishes Emma still lived round the corner. But Emma moved back to Glasgow after her wedding and now she's incapable of FaceTiming without Jamie. And Juliet loves Jamie. But every time Juliet tries to speak to Emma, Jamie is *there*.

'That's good. That's good, because the justice system is so fucked, don't you think? Like, oh . . . victim of sexual violence, are you? How about some *state* violence, as well?' Oscar runs his thick fingers through his well-groomed beard.

'I feel a bit guilty, though. About . . . not doing anything,' says Juliet. 'I feel like I'm supposed to do something.'

'You will, though,' Oscar says. 'You could shame him on social media, or . . . There must be like, a *racists getting fired* type of thing for sex criminals.'

'I think that's just like . . . the Sex Offenders' Register, isn't it?'

'You wouldn't have to call him out on your account.' He completely ignores her half-joke. 'In fact, we could do it more like . . . more like a whisper network. Or I could message my friend from that feminist book club, the one with all the Instagram followers. Get them to name and shame him,' he says. He looks at Juliet expectantly. She gets the sense he has thought about this before. Oscar has lain awake at night and thought about what he would do if one of his friends was raped; how he could *sort it out* without phoning the police.

Juliet recalls a night out from a few years ago. Some man had grabbed Hannah's arse on their way out of the club, and Hannah didn't tell them what had happened until they were all in the taxi home. Oscar picked an argument with her. Juliet and Hannah were sat in the back of the cab, while Oscar lectured from the front seat – *I could have said something to him,* he'd insisted. *I wouldn't have let him get away with it.*

'I don't think I want to make a spectacle of myself like that,' says Juliet.

'No. Of course not. You're more of a *direct-action* girl, aren't you?' says Oscar, presumably referring to the time Juliet egged a red-faced EDL marcher at a counter-protest shortly before they were moved on by police. Oscar had repeatedly told her, *I wish I'd thrown something.* He had sulked all day. 'We could confront him.'

'Oscar . . .' Juliet says. 'I don't want you to do anything. I just wanted to talk about it.'

'Okay,' says Oscar. 'I'm sorry.'

They drink and Oscar looks for a harmless film to put on, something devoid of upsetting content. He puts on *Wayne's World*, and they drink more wine. His leg bounces up and down and he keeps looking over at Juliet like he's annoyed. He keeps looking at his phone.

'He's in the Crown and Anchor right now,' says Oscar. The Crown is around the corner. A ten-minute walk, at most. 'I just saw it on his Instagram story. I just went to block him, but my thumb slipped.' He shakes his head. 'I'm going to say something.'

He stamps over to his shoes piled in the corner; pulls on a heavy pair of DMs he calls his *kicking boots*.

Juliet's backpack is in a heap by Oscar's shoes. A plastic button reading *kill your local rapist* glints at her, calls her a *poser*.

'Are you coming with me? You don't have to.' Oscar zips up his jacket. Juliet says she'll come.

They walk to the pub and Juliet feels as if she has left her soul behind on the sofa. Her body trails behind Oscar, on automatic pilot.

'What are you going to do?' Juliet asks.

Oscar doesn't hear her. He's walking a little ahead of her. His legs are much longer than hers, and he doesn't seem to notice that he's leaving her behind.

When they enter the pub, Oscar buys them both pints. He doesn't ask Juliet what she wants, if she wants, he just puts the lager in her hands. He drinks his in a few greedy mouthfuls *bracing himself*, slamming the empty glass on the bar before he stalks the pub like an eager dog looking for his ball. Juliet slops beer over her hands as she tries to keep up.

They find the rapist upstairs, playing pool. He looks at Oscar and Juliet, and smiles. He waves them over. He winks at Juliet.

'Hey, trouble,' he says. Juliet watches Oscar and says nothing. Her heart is hammering, her throat is tight. She shakes so much that she can almost feel her bones rattling. 'Are you okay?'

'She'll be fine,' says Oscar. Oscar looks back at Juliet, expectantly. He is avuncular, urging a shy child to say hello. 'Won't you?'

She shrugs. She sips her pint.

'Can I have a word, Juliet?' says the rapist. 'About the other night,' he adds. 'You didn't answer my messages.'

'She doesn't want to speak to you,' snaps Oscar.

'Er . . .' The rapist looks to Juliet for backup, smirks, *Get a load of this guy*. 'Right. No offence, pal, but this is none of your business?' The rapist puts down his pool cue and takes a step towards Juliet. Oscar stands in front of her, blocking her with his bulk. Juliet can't seem to do anything but sip her pint.

'I'm making it my business,' says Oscar. The people with the rapist are not paying attention to this exchange. Juliet recognises some of them; there's Sarah-from-Work's boyfriend, the barista from her favourite coffee shop, a tattoo artist she's friendly with. No women, though. 'She told me what you did.'

The rapist's smirk shatters, twists; he glares at Juliet.

'What I *did*?' says the rapist. 'The fuck does that mean?'

Oscar grabs a half-empty can of Red Stripe and chucks it at the rapist, hitting him in the chest, spattering beer everywhere. The rapist drops his half-empty pint, which shatters at his feet.

Oscar rushes him, and the rapist catches Oscar in his arms. They embrace like boxers in the middle of a prize bout; it is almost tender. Oscar easily overpowers the rapist, who is a far smaller man, still blinking beer from his eyes.

Juliet has never seen Oscar successfully get in a fight – she's seen him square up to people before, and his size always defuses the confrontation. Now, he knocks the rapist to the ground and pummels him, clumsily among the glass and the beer.

Juliet cannot tell how hard Oscar is hitting the rapist, but a string of bloody spit lands on her white trainers. The rapist's friends only now seem to clock that something is going on, and Sarah's boyfriend and the barista remove Oscar, demanding to know what the fuck he's playing at. The rapist spits out a bloody mass of pulp and broken tooth at Juliet's feet.

She imagines herself, cartoonishly empowered, stamping her foot on the rapist's nose. She imagines bones crushed beneath the sole of her shoe, cartilage popping, horror movie blood splatter. She imagines kicking his teeth in. She imagines stamping on his throat. She imagines putting her hands down his trousers and ripping off his testicles.

Still, she cannot bring herself to move.

Oscar struggles free of the rapist's cronies.

'He raped her.' Oscar is pointing at Juliet, as if he were accusing her. 'Didn't he, Juliet?'

Juliet is staring at the fragment of tooth near her feet. She nods, weakly.

'No,' says the rapist. 'No, wasn't like that,' he says. 'I . . . She . . .' He sits up, drooling blood, and grabs the leg of her jeans. 'You *know* it wasn't like that, Jules.'

She jerks her leg away. She knows *exactly* what it was like. She doesn't know what to say. In a few hours, she will be kicking herself, thinking about the snappy fuck-you comebacks she could have hit him with. She knows this moment will bury itself into her brain, that it will live more clearly in her memory than the rape itself.

Oscar stamps on the rapist's fingers.

'Let's go, Juliet.' He plucks her pint from her hands, and tips its remainder over the rapist's head. Oscar drags her from the pub, back to their home.

They sit on the sofa and ice his swollen fists with a bag of frozen peas. Juliet is on the verge of a panic attack. She is a balloon filling with air, stretching to burst.

'Christ, I feel so much better,' Oscar says. 'He won't be doing that again, will he?' Oscar seems to expect a response from Juliet; he looks up at her with a small smile on his face. 'Will he?'

Juliet has a text from Sarah-from-Work, simply reading:

> what the fuuuuuuuck jules?!??!?!?!

And then a moment later:

> Fuck nvm I just got more deets from bf, im so sorry

> But also what the fuck??

> Oscar??????

Hyper-aware now of the speed at which this will spread through their wider friendship group, Juliet gets a DM on Instagram from both the tattoo artist and the barista. The tattoo artist's message begins: *hey really sorry* whereas the barista's opens, and likely closes, with: *mental fucking bitch*.

Her phone pings again, and again.

'Whoa,' says Oscar. 'What's that about?'

She's Always Hungry

Thou shalt have a fishy
on a little dishy
Thou shalt have a fishy
when the boat comes in

★

'Play it again, and I'll gut you,' said our Mary's Samuel. He had his knife in my face, and he tried to slam the lid of the piano down upon my fingers. I pulled back my hands before they were crushed, like a hermit crab beneath a shoe.

The pub was lively tonight, but I was not. I was dragged along. I did not want to drink or play darts, or weep over lost brothers. The pub was claustrophobic – once a cottage like any other in the village; I felt anxious when all of us were crammed inside of it. I went to the piano so I could sit quietly on my own, keep my hands busy with something other than drink. I could only play one song, so I played it over and over again.

'Mary Mountjoy's Sammy doesn't want his fishy,' said Violet Fisher's Daniel.

'Our Kitty's John has played that flaming song *fifty* flaming times, and I won't hear it again,' said our Mary's Sam. He turned his ire back to me. 'You trying to wind us up?'

'No. It's the only tune I can play off the top of my head,' I said. I did not care for my cousin, who was rough and quick to anger. He did not care for me, because I was meek and mild – a mother's pet.

'Then let someone who can play properly have it,' he said. Our Mary's Sam pulled me up and away from the piano by the collar of my shirt. 'Where's Rosie Andrews' John?'

Rosie Andrews' John got up from his table with his pint and a mean smirk. He played piano well, but he loved to prod a sharp stick into a soft spot. He opened the lid of the piano, and keeping his eyes to our Mary's Sam, he played, and sang loudly.

Come here my little Jacky
Now I've smoked my baccy
Let's have a bit of cracky
till the boat comes in

'Dance to thy nanny,' sang Rosie Andrews' John. 'Sing to thy mammy.' He was laughing, and the rest of the pub joined. We all laughed at our Mary's Samuel. Our Mary's Samuel went red as guts. He stomped towards the door with his knife still drawn.

'You off home, then?' I asked.

'Off away from yous. Wind-up merchants, the lot of you,' he said. He was one-foot out the door – then, a snigger. He stopped, turned around, marched back over to Rosie Andrews' John and stuck the knife in his back. I don't think it had been Rosie Andrews' John who'd laughed, but it seemed like Our Mary's Samuel was past the point of sensible thought, growling like something rabid, like he wanted to stick his little knife into each and everyone of us. Betty Hardy's David took the initiative – smashed a glass over Our Mary's Sam, bloodied his head, knocked him to the floor.

We tied his hands and took him to the Mothers. We dragged him through the village, past all the little cottages. Some of our good women looked out from their windows and doors. They shook their heads but did not ask what we were up to. Men's nonsense, they knew.

All the cottages were arranged in circles around the Mothers' longhouse – our Mary's Sammy was spared no dignity on his journey.

We rapped on the door and were greeted by Mother Perch – who was unmoved and unimpressed. She ushered us inside with a click of her tongue.

'I told you all,' she said to the other Mothers. 'We should shut that pub when the sea's rough. *A rough sea—*'

'*Wets a man's brain*, we know,' clucked our Mother Mountjoy, as she scooped up our Mary's Samuel.

Mother White tended to Rosie Andrews' John's back, while Mother Andrews saw to our Mary's Samuel. She called our Mother Mountjoy to come over. He was still unconscious and the top of his head was wet with blood. He was balled up on the wooden floor, twitching. Mother Andrews and our Mother Mountjoy moved him to a rug.

Mothers Hardy and Perch spoke in hushed tones – I could tell they were arguing about the pub. They did not like the fights the alcohol brought, and they did not trust a space with no women there to keep things under control. But it seemed that it was good for us; the men seemed happier when we had a place to be with one another.

Having seen the bickering, the drinking, the violence first hand – I did not trust the pub. I would not defy our Mother, but inside of myself, I agreed with Mother Perch.

Our Mother snapped her fingers in front of my face and scolded me for eavesdropping.

'Why did you have to wind up our Sammy, so?' our Mother asked me.

'I didn't know he was getting annoyed, Mother. I can only play the one song.'

'I'd think hearing any song enough times would drive a man mad,' said Mother Fisher. She was the oldest Mother. She was also the smallest and her hair was the longest and whitest. Violet Fisher's Daniel spoke up for me.

'If I can, Mother . . . and Mother Mountjoy – your Kitty's John really only played the song a few times – then it was Rosie Andrews' John that pushed him over the edge.'

We looked over to Rosie Andrews' John, and he nodded.

'I was winding him up, I'll admit to that. But not so

much I deserved a knife.' We all nodded, all the men. 'With all due respect, I think it was your Mary's Sammy who was in the wrong.' He hissed while Mother White worked the little knife from his shoulder. 'In my opinion, anyway.'

The Mothers looked at one another. They made faces at each other, and they made gestures with their hands. Mother White shrugged, and Mother Perch clicked her tongue. None of them seemed happy with one another. I got the sense they wanted us, the men, to leave.

Our Mother sighed. She bent down to our Mary's Sam, and picked a small piece of glass from his hair. He was still knocked out, still bleeding.

'Well, we'd best get my Mary. And,' she looked over to Mother Andrews, 'best fetch your Rosie, too.'

They sent me to fetch Rosie Andrews and our Mary. I got them together and explained what had happened. I was worried they would be angry at me once I told them I'd been playing the song too much. But they said I had no need to worry, nothing to apologise for.

Then they apologised to one another on behalf of their sons. Our Mary said her Sammy's got a vile temper, and Rosie Andrews said her John's a little wind-up merchant and might well have deserved it. I led them to the long-house and thought about how wise the women were. They forgave each other and they even forgave each other's men. They always thought the best of each other.

The covenant of men was fickle; we fought and blamed and had no time or patience for each other's follies. We saw ill intent and malice where there was none. We strived to be good for the women, but we failed. We fail because we are born with a lungful of seawater; like the sea we are mercurial and cruel.

At the longhouse, our Mother asked our Mary how our Sammy had been lately. Had he been irritable, or distracted? Did he seem distant? Hadn't he gone under a few weeks prior? Hadn't he fallen in the sea?

Our Mary looked worried.

'Should we get him deaf?' she asked.

'We haven't gotten a man deaf since my Daniel sixty years hence. It didn't work. It didn't contain the spread, it just drove him mad,' said Mother Fisher.

'Then what?' our Mary asked.

'We shouldn't talk about this in front of the boys,' said Mother Fisher.

Mother Hardy took me and Rosie Andrews' John outside. She admired the stitching on Rosie Andrews' John's back, then told us to be good, and slapped us both on the wrist.

★

I didn't know why they'd want to get a man deaf, but I knew my place and did not ask questions. If the Mothers wanted us to know something, they'd tell us. That was good enough for me. I was one of the best boys – people were always telling my mammy that – and I protected that reputation. As much as I worked for it, I was good by nature, too. I had always been a good boy.

Despite my youth, the other men have looked to me as a peacemaker. Some even said I could have come just from my mother alone, with no man's blood or seed inside to spoil me. I was told the man who had fathered me was meek and gentle; I was well-bred. I was told that he had long since gone to the sea and that his name was also John; but I can't remember which Mother he belonged to – so he is as good as lost to me.

Our Mary's Samuel was not well-bred, my mother often told me. Our Mary was too impatient for a daughter, and she did not put in the effort to negotiate with the mother of a good man to get one. Though our Mary had three children – her Samuel and her Brogan and her Melinda – my mammy had only me. I was born too late for her to have another. It was a disappointment not to have a girl. But she didn't want to put a bad man out into the world. Being the mother to a bad man was a worse sin than being daughterless.

'My sacrifice is lauded,' Mammy told me. 'And our Mary's greed for daughters making up a bad son has been noted by the Mothers. She'll never see a day as head of our house.'

The Mothers told us we would not see our Mary's Samuel for several days, so Mammy sent me to get fish for our Mary, and her Brogan and Melinda.

I went out on the boat with a net, and Rosie Andrews' John came out to help. It was a gentle day, but our Brogan told me to be careful and not to go too far out on the water.

'Don't feel the need to overfish for us. If the weather

turns, come back to me,' she said. 'I'll be here on the shore with a line.'

'Thank you,' I told her.

'And the same goes for you, Rosie's John.'

We got on a little boat, and we watched our Brogan set up her fishing pole as we paddled out. We watched her get smaller, and smaller, as we floated further out to sea. We did as we were told and did not go out too far. We set out the net and hauled up fish.

Rosie Andrews' John asked me if I knew what was wrong with Mary Mountjoy's Samuel.

'If the Mothers needed us to know—'

'They'd tell us. I know that. But we're out of their earshot for the time. So, what do *you* know? Or what do you *think*? If you don't know nowt.'

'I don't know nowt I'm not supposed to, and I don't think owt about it.'

'Well do you want me to tell you what I know? Because I know things. My mammy's brother told me, you know, our Maggie's Gerald.'

Maggie Andrews' Gerald had a high status among men, on account of the fact he had lived to be over sixty before the sea took him. He was a mentor and helper to many of us. He was gentle. And because of his nature and his long life he was often privy to knowledge that many men would not live to collect.

I did not say anything. My curiosity fought with my desire to be pure of anything I had not been given by our

Mothers. The machinations of men had done so little for this place, and for the world outside of here.

'There's something in the water here that takes the men,' he said.

'We all go to the water eventually.'

'Not the water itself, dafty, something *in* the water. Something what calls out to us, and drives us mad, and takes us.'

'We've all heard tell of finwives luring fishermen from their women, and those are just children's stories.'

'*No*,' said Rosie Andrews' John. 'You're not listening to me. Because this isn't some finwife or siren story. It's not some folk tale. It's in your head. It gets in your head and brings you down with it. Maybe to make you a slave—'

'Sounds an awful lot like a finwife story.'

'—maybe to eat you. We don't know. Our Maggie's Gerald said that we'd lost a lot of men that way – some women, too. Sometimes, getting bred helped rid the afflicted. But any babe born by a man or woman with that thing inside their head came out wrong – with gills.'

'I've never seen a baby with gills.'

'They put them in the water. They swim away.'

I winced when he talked about breeding. I tried not to think about it. Men who thought too much about getting bred became strange and disrespectful with their eyes. They tried to lure good women into secret trysts that their mothers did not know about. I looked over to our Brogan on the rock and I saw her reeling in a fish. She was paying us no mind and certainly could not hear us, but voices carry on the wind.

'I feel sorry for your Rosie Andrews, you know. Because that is one of the most wetbrained things I've ever been told. I think if my son was coming out with such a salty mess as that, I'd send him out to sea with a net and hope he got stuck in it,' I said. Rosie Andrews' John glared at me.

'I heard you reeled in something funny last week, *John*,' he hissed. 'I heard you was on the water alone, and you reeled in something *dead* funny.'

I smacked him, so he punched me hard in the arm. I lost my balance, and I fell from the boat.

I had fallen from much bigger boats into much rougher seas, so I did not panic. I tried to let myself float upwards, but my ankle was caught in our net. And while I was under, I heard it whisper to me. I heard it clear as day, as if there were no water there to catch the words. I heard my catch of the day, calling to me from where I was keeping it.

John John John John John John John John John John John John John John John John

A chorus. Rosie Andrews' John pulled me up, and when I surfaced, I could hear our Brogan shouting from the rock.

We came back to the shore with a boat full of fish, and our Brogan slapped our wrists for fighting. She sent Rosie Andrews' John home and had me warm up by the fire while she gutted fish. Our Melinda deboned them, and our Mary salted them. They had me take the fish out to their smokehouse, where I hung them up to dry.

★

'Our Mary said you fell in the water,' said Mammy. At home, she was writing at her desk. I'm not sure what she was writing – but it was likely to do with the organisation of the village stores for the winter. She was important, and always told me these things did not concern me, so I did not ask. She rose from the desk and smelled me. 'Too much fish stink on you for my liking,' she said. She sent me to the bath with a little bottle of lavender oil.

I could not be bothered to warm the water, so I sat in the bath behind the cottage in cold water pumped straight from the tap. I dripped in the lavender oil, and hoped it would kill the smell of fish and seawater. I thought about my catch of the day. And I thought about wetbrained Rosie Andrews' John, and I thought about his stupid story. And I found myself unable to draw a line in my head between the two: between my catch of the day and Rosie Andrews' John's story.

My catch of the day could not be some siren because it did not speak. It did not look like a man or a woman so it could not be finfolk. It did not even have a mouth.

I was quiet at dinner and Mammy was worried. She asked me if I was nervous about my first big fishing trip – if I was worried about getting taken out on the big boat at this time of year. And I told her that I was. She told me that all men must go to the sea eventually, and she smiled.

'But I hope you'll live to spring,' she said. 'Might be a breeding season.' I twisted my face, and she patted my arm affectionately. 'The Mothers said I might be able to claim a granddaughter,' she said. 'If you sire more than one.'

'Yes, Mammy,' I said. I poked at the potatoes my mammy had made me.

'You're such a good boy,' she said.

★

After Mammy went to bed, I went to see my catch. I could not keep it in the house. I am unsure why. I just knew that it would not be possible. Nor could it go in the cellar because Mammy's down there all the time. Though I hide nothing from my mammy – I hid my catch of the day. A curious compulsion I was unable to unpick.

I took it to an old fisher's shack. We have them all over the coast; little shacks with a cot and some preserves inside. They're useful if you're night fishing or lost and on your own. Sometimes you open a shack, and pull out a wheezing, half-drowned man; sometimes you find a desiccated corpse or a pile of bones, and you have to check his clothes to see if his mother's name is sewn into them.

The old shack – where I left my catch – was tucked alongside the cliffs that bordered our land; the place where the sandy beach gave way to jagged, slippery rocks. The shack was rusty, with a hole in the roof. There was no mattress on the cot, and no preserves left inside. I knew of it (as did a handful of others) as a place to hide secrets. Stolen objects, stolen kisses – I had never used it before

32

– but our Brogan took me here once as a little boy. She showed me a small knife she had stashed here, then grabbed my arm and cut it. My skin parted like butter. As I approached the shack, I rolled up my sleeve. Though it was dark, I could see the bumpy old scar on my arm. The cut got infected because the knife was dirty. After a day, the wound was yellow, and weepy. It was salted and cleaned but it still healed wrong. The scar was fat, shiny and white, like a worm curling around my forearm. I never told no one our Brogan did it. I said I fell down.

I could hear the sea, and I could hear my own name. Both became louder as I walked towards my catch. *John John John John John John* and the crash of waves. Upon the door of the shack was a hastily scrawled sign, one I had written and hung myself.

KEEP OUT – UNSAFE STRUCTURE

I entered. And tangled in a net atop the bare frame of the cot was my catch of the day.

I would not call it a merman or a mermaid. I would not call it a siren or a selkie, or finfolk or bucca, because it did not seem human enough to be any of those. But it was too human to simply be some enormous fish. It had a person's torso. It was small: womanly at the waist and breast, but masculine at the shoulders. It had arms that looked to me like the legs of goats or horses. I would not say that it had hands – but it did have fingers.

It had a long, slippery tail – more like an eel's than something a fish would have because it was serpentine and frilled. It didn't have fins or scales; it was totally hairless and moist and spongy to the touch. Its entire body was hagfish slippery; smooth and cased in a thin slick of mucus.

It was mouthless and noseless; it had gills ribbing its neck and what I supposed was its jaw. Its head was dominated by two huge, black eyes: clear, jellyfish domes over deep black pits. They were delicate, and endless; they shimmered and glittered in the light like the moon on the water.

When I first pulled it up into my boat, I was afraid. And then I was not, because I knew that it was *my* catch. My thing. I would be able to keep it forever and admire it. I thought about butchering it and eating it, so it could be within me forever. I thought about making its bones into little trinkets. Then I did not think that any more – like a door had slammed closed on the thought. Instead, I thought the creature itself could be my slippery trinket, living and breathing and in my arms.

I thought about untangling it from the net, but I was too frightened it would leave me. I had rowed it to the shack, and fastened the net to the bed frame.

'Hello,' I said. I dropped down to its level and inspected it. The net was beginning to cut into its flesh. I touched its tail. It now felt dry to the touch. 'I think I can hear you.'

lovely John hungry John John John hungry John hungry John

'You're hungry?' I asked. And it flexed its tail. 'What do you eat?'

the sea eat the sea the things the sea in the sea suck suck suck the sea in the sea eat eat eat eat eat in sea

I decided to bring it a basin to sit in, one I'd fill with seawater. There was an old tin bath in our cellar, one I'd used as a boy and grown out of. I would take that and bring it tomorrow.

no no tomorrow sea now in the sea the eat in the sea eat eat

So I did not wait till the next day. I brought the bath and filled it with seawater. I dragged it into the shack and proceeded to untangle the catch from its net. I picked it up from the floor like a child and lowered it into the water. It shuddered, and the water turned pink. I petted its tail; it became slicker and slicker the more I touched it.

good sea good touch sing song sing song sing song

I sang to it.

> Thou shalt have a fishy
> on a little dishy
> Thou shalt have a fishy
> when the boat comes in

It swayed when I sang. It shuddered. If it had had hands to clap, I imagine it would.

I left before sunrise.

35

The men take the biggest boats out for the pre-winter fishing trip. It is a trip to catch as much fish as we can to hang and smoke and dry for our winter stores. It is a dangerous venture, and we sometimes lose as many as ten men.

In November we make the trip, and the women spend the rest of the month gutting and drying the fish. In January, the pregnant women who ascended to the mid-wife's hall the previous summer would come down from the hill with new babies. They would be presented with extra provisions, the barrels containing the biggest and best catches.

This would be my first pre-winter fishing trip. We had to prepare, and the women had to manage our preparations. Our Mother Mountjoy was overseeing our work. We were stocking the boat with safe things to drink, and lemons, and dried fish and fruit. But also tools, rope, nets, harpoons, knives. I was hauling a barrel of fish that was too big for my small body. I was yawning and swaying on my feet. Our Mother Mountjoy came to me and stroked her hands through my hair.

'Sleep badly, pet?' she asked. I nodded. She had me rest. I sat with her and watched the other men continue with their tasks. I saw Bess Perch's Andrew crack open the barrel of lemons he was dragging and begin to eat them like apples.

'I'm starving,' he said. And then a few more men

followed suit. They opened their barrels and began to eat. Our Mother Mountjoy whistled, and more men came to control their hungry brothers. Their mouths were smeared with fish bits and fruit pulp.

'Take them to the longhouse,' she said. 'Take them away.'

Many of the men looked frightened and confused, but Mother was calm. She told them to go back to work, and not to worry. I was worried.

'Little pet,' she asked. 'Have you heard tell of any strange catches lately? Any especially big fish?'

'No, Mother,' I said. I had to restrain myself from clapping my hand over my mouth, because I had never lied to her before. I wanted to tell her the truth, and then I did not.

'Have you heard owt? Anything odd about?' She took my hand. Her skin was crinkled and papery.

'No, Mother, nowt strange since our Mary's Samuel at the pub.'

She sighed.

'No. A good boy like you wouldn't know. I'll have to find a bad man to ask, won't I?'

'Yes, Mother.'

'Yes, I will.'

She did not send me back to work. She held my hand. She was my great-grandmother. She told me I was her favourite boy – she had twenty-five great-grandchildren, and ten of us were boys, and I was her best one. I wanted to cry, and I wanted to tell her the truth. But then I did not. And then I felt fine.

37

The men began to sing as they worked.

> Dance for thy nanny
> Sing for thy mammy
> Dance for thy nanny
> when the boat comes in

★

When next I saw my catch, its voice was clearer inside my head. No longer a collection of words – a vague sense of something being said – I heard a woman's voice.

Hello John, I heard, *Hello hello hello John I would like a change of seawater PLEASE THANK YOU John*

So I brought it a change of water, and I listened to the things it told me. I was not able to contemplate its new voice – why it had changed.

You are a good and nice boy for bringing me new water how good it is to be a nice good boy are there other good nice boys here could they come and say hello could they be a friend to me could they bring me new water more you could bring them or I could bring them I could bring the boys or you could bring the boys but nice good boys your good women cannot hear me only your good men so I would like to see them and I would like you to sing me the song about the fishy and the dishy thank you PLEASE thank please you

When it spoke to me, I could not hear my own thoughts. I could not feel myself, only the catch of the day. I sank into what it was telling me. I closed my eyes, and I heard its

38

voice, and I came back to myself and found that the catch was splashing happily in new water, and I could hear my own voice singing it the song. Our song, now.

I noticed that the catch now had a mouth: a long slit along its face. And its arms had changed – the joints were more like elbows than knees. Its fingers were not as long; it seemed to be growing palms.

I was weak I was sick but you are making me better good nice boy I get stronger more pretty for you John like a pretty pretty yes a pretty for John and a good touch for the CATCH OF THE DAY.

I began to pet its tail. Her tail.

*

She continued to change. Each night I came back to something slightly more human. Her eyes were smaller, her skin was less slippery and softer. Full lips formed around the new slit of her mouth, but she did not speak to me with it because it did not seem to open. An ersatz nose formed at the centre of her face – a little point. After a week, the catch of the day began to resemble a woman. A human woman, with silvery skin, and big black eyes.

I think you're the best boy here, John. I think you're the best boy.

*

I was helping Mammy in the kitchen when it occurred to me that I had not seen or heard of my cousin since the stabbing.

I had forgotten about him – completely forgotten. Mammy and I were kneading bread together in silence, so I broke it. I asked her if she'd heard news of our Mary's Samuel.

'Oh,' she said. 'I wouldn't worry about him.' Then she said: 'You look a bit thin, pet. Are you well?'

'Yes, Mammy,' I said.

'Why don't you go to the pub. You must need to relax. All the work you've been doing. It seems like you're not sleeping well. I hear you up at night.'

'Yes, Mammy.'

'All the men are going to the pub tonight, I hear. You should go as well.'

I washed the flour from my hands as Mammy brushed it from my clothes. She walked me to the pub and said I should stay as long as I wanted. She did not go back the way we came, instead walking towards the longhouse.

I watched her for a moment, then opened the door to the pub. The men inside were singing.

> Thou shalt have a fishy
> on a little dishy
> Thou shalt have a fishy
> when the boat comes in

They were all standing up and swaying to the song. They were not dancing. They swayed on the spot like pendulums. Someone was playing the piano but not really. He was banging the keys in a rough approximation of the tune.

I felt guilty and panicked and then I did not. When I entered the pub the singing stopped; the men all said my name (alone, without my mother's) and clapped. They told me I was the best boy.

But then one of the older men – Jane White's David – let out this awful wail.

'He's not the best boy,' he said. 'I am. I'm the best boy.' The other men booed and some of them hit him.

'JOHN IS THE BEST BOY,' they chorused.

Jane White's David shook his head. The men began to descend upon him. He was a small man and wiggled free, and he ran from them, past me, out of the door of the pub. I realised where he was going. I knew he was going to *her*. To *my* thing.

So, I followed him. And the other men began to follow, too, but they all halted – they were like wind-up toys with no wind left in them. They stopped still in the doorway of the pub as I ran after Jane White's David. He was older than me but so much faster.

We ran through the village, ran past all the little cottages, ran to the beach and towards the shack.

'You'll stop that,' I shouted, breathless. 'Jane White's David, you'll stop.'

'No,' he said. 'Because I'm the best boy and I'm going to go to it.'

'To what?' I called. He looked over his shoulder, brow crinkled.

'I don't know! But I'm going.'

41

And we continued to run till he arrived at the shack. I began to hear her, and I could no longer see. Or at least, I could no longer fully make sense of what I saw. I could see, but I could no longer understand it; as if I were looking at a book and had forgotten how to read. But I heard her.

Oh dear! I thought this might be a good man, yes? But obviously not. A good boy would not come in here without asking me or you first, no? What if he steals me? What if he puts me in danger? What if he were to put his filthy little hands upon my sweet wet body? No, no, no, no, no, no, no, John, we couldn't have that. No thank you please, John!

And when I could see again, Jane White's David was dead. It was the middle of the night, and I had disassembled him, and she was ripping apart one of his hands, and dropping chunks of flesh into the bathwater. I was also dropping chunks of flesh into the bathwater. His leg was in my lap, and I was stripping it with a knife.

She had become more human, and more beautiful. She had breasts with no teats, and she was covered in blood. Her mouth did not open but it was rosier; it was curled into a soft little smile.

All the men will say that he ran into the sea and that you went after him to help. You should take off all your clothes and get in the sea. And then you should go to your women's longhouse and you should tell them about it. All the men are good boys now and they'll tell the women the same thing. It will be all easy and no trouble. The women are up

to something so you know. Up to something bad. I hear a
little just a little from them and they are up to something.

She looked at me and dropped the rest of the hand into
the water. She squeezed the new breasts with her fully
formed hands, as if offering them to me, wanting to know
if I liked them. I did not dislike the breasts. But I did not
know what she wanted me to do with them. I did not have
any interest in this sort of thing. In breasts. In looking at
them, and in doing so disrespectfully.

Very good. That's a very good boy.

★

I did as I was told. I left all my clothes with her, and I got
into the sea. I walked back to the village. I was freezing and
my body was nearly blue by the time I arrived at the longhouse. All the women were there, not just the Mothers. My
own mammy came to me and wrapped me in a large rug.
She walked me over to the fire.

I told the women what the catch of the day had told me
to say. My mammy and all the Mountjoy women fussed
over me. While Jane White wept and shook; the White
women fussed over her. The Andrewses, the Perches, the
Hardys and the Fishers looked on, murmuring in confusion
and concern.

'It's happening again,' announced Mother Hardy. 'One
of the finfolk is in our midst.'

'But the finfolk aren't real,' I told Mammy.

'No,' she said. 'Perhaps not in the way the stories make

43

it seem. But there are a people in the sea. We call them the finfolk for that is the best word we have for them. And they are . . . dangerous.'

'*Kitty Mountjoy*,' snapped Mother White. 'You'll not tell that boy another word.'

'We'll have to tell them soon enough, Mother White,' said Mammy. 'We'll have to hunt it out. We'll need every pair of hands we have, and if my lad seems well enough, we'll need him.'

I saw the women argue for the first time. Mother White said that no man could be trusted in the presence of the finfolk. No man could resist their call, and it was said that even some women could not resist, either. Mother White's words were barbed and tipped with poisonous suspicion. The Whites and the Hardys cheered, '*Hear, hear!*' And then my mammy looked at me without love or trust. Under her eye I felt like a stale loaf of bread – a disappointment, to be inspected for rot and discarded.

Our Mother Mountjoy asked me what the men had been like at the pub tonight. I did not know what to say.

'They were normal,' I blurted. 'I thought everything was normal. Maybe Jane White's David was the only man who was . . . affected?'

'There's never just one,' said our Mother Mountjoy.

★

At home, my mammy put me to bed. She told me not to worry about what the other women said. She told me I was

44

a brave man for going after Jane White's David. She tucked me in and kissed my forehead.

I fell asleep quickly. I was tired. In my dreams the catch of the day came to me – she did not have a tail any more, but a pair of malformed legs. She had long stringy hair, like seaweed.

To serve me then be consumed by me is the greatest joy. Your mother does not love you, you are just a thrall to her. You are a servant and a sack of seed from which might spring a granddaughter. But I love you. I love you very much. They cannot deny you the ecstasy you'll find inside me.

I woke up angry. For the first time, I woke up angry. I went to stand but could not because I was tied to the bed.

Mammy and the Mothers were in my room, gathered around my bed. Our Mother Mountjoy pulled back my eyelids, and Mother Fisher peered into my eyes. Mother Perch searched my body. Mammy asked:

'How long have you been in cahoots with the creature?'

'I'm not.'

'We found the shack,' Mother White said.

'The sign on the door was in your handwriting,' said Mammy. 'And we know it's new, because our Brogan said she'd been to the shack two weeks ago. And there was no creature, and no sign.'

'It's not my writing,' I said.

'Don't lie to me,' said Mammy. 'I taught you to write, don't think I don't recognise your hand.'

'You've never loved me,' I said. 'I'm just a thrall to you and a servant and a sack of seed.'

'And the creature does love you? You're a son to her?' asked Mother Andrews. I nodded.

'To serve her then be consumed by her is the greatest joy,' I said. I expected the Mothers to look shocked, or afraid or impressed. Instead, they looked at each other like I'd said something very stupid. 'You will not deny me the ecstasy I would find inside her.'

'I always said you spoilt this boy, Kitty,' said Mother Hardy. And then she struck me on the head, and I went back to sleep. I did not hear the catch of the day – I suppose because no part of my mind was conscious.

I woke again and found myself slung over Rosie Andrews' John's back. He was taking me to the beach. The women were waiting for us and so were the men. The women stood, and the men sat cross-legged at their feet, like little children. Rosie Andrews' John dropped me on the sand in front of a pyre and sat with the others. They intended to burn me, it seemed.

'Let this be a lesson,' said our Mother Mountjoy. 'About showing any man too much leniency. Let this be a lesson: not a single man is to be trusted – even the meekest, sweetest boy. Not a single one.'

The women applauded. The men sat silently. Then stood. The Mothers did not notice at first, because they were attempting to light the pyre. But the other women did. They clucked, and urged the men to sit back down, but they did not. At first the men were calm. They walked purposefully and slowly towards the sea. And when the Mothers said: 'Grab your men,' they ran. They ran into the sea. A great wave swallowed them and dragged them away. The women screamed, but from the sea, there was an eerie silence.

Then the women followed. I saw our Mary, and Jane White. Most of the younger women, too. They ran to the ocean.

The Mothers and the handful of remaining women stopped looking at the sea. All of them old, north of sixty, I realised. We had no men north of sixty.

Then it was as if they had all remembered I was here at once – they all turned towards me. I scuttled backwards. I tried to will my catch of the day to save me. I begged her to come for me. And then I saw her. Tucked among the women – the only young face among them. She was hiding her new legs under a long dress. She was there, and she was looking at me, and smirking with her false mouth. Even these old women who resisted the pull of the sea were blind to her. I begged them to look at her.

Well, John, I heard. *We had a good run, you and I. Perhaps you'll see me again. Perhaps you could join me in the sea one day. Perhaps you'll die by fire. I will be busy with your brothers and your women; this is a fine meal for me and mine, you see, a fine fine fine fine fine meal yes we'll be very full.*

Then I heard nothing.

The ringing stopped. I had been hearing it since I caught her, hadn't I? And I had not noticed it. I had not noticed this incessant, painful, high-pitched ringing which had rendered me half deaf for a fortnight. It was like a music box, the tune:

> Thou shalt have a fishy
> on a little dishy
> Thou shalt have a fishy
> when the boat comes in

The women advanced on me.

The Shadow Over Little Chitaly

☆ – SUE IN ROTHERHAM
CALL ME BACK WANT REFUND
*Mustve been listed on justeat for my area by mistake as
came from 125 miles away??? pizza was just plain base
but with the entire flipping chinese served on top of it??
not what i ordered wtf. cant get hold of the restaurant for
a refund have rang 117 times.*

☆☆☆ – CARYS IN SWANSEA
APPLE?
*Thoroughly edible, if a bit cold/late (had apparently
come from 43 miles away – your guess is as good as
mine) but the Hawaiian pizza came with apple instead of
pineapple.*

☆ – HANNAH IN CLITHEROE
SPECIAL PIZZA, DONT DO IT
*Looked at here once or twice. Was curious but never fully
enticed by the idea of a takeaway that's half Chinese and*

half Italian. Just makes you think both are gunna be a bit shit or the Chinese will be good and pizzas very shit, or vice versa. Had a look and noticed a new pizza: Chitaly Special. Gone from the menu now but here's the text (took a screenshot)

```
LIMITED - Chitaly special pizza
G'day mates! Enjoy ALL the flavours of china ALL
the flavours of Italy try it and do not regret
this treat straight from the barbie. The cuisine
secrets of the Italian east and the china west
together in cheesy harmony yum yum!
```

And I thought. Alright then. Fuck me up Chitaly. Even after greeted with a checkbox for a 'Boneless' option, I went for it. Nothing but regret.
Will try to describe what arrived at my door. First it practically teleported here, must have only taken about 10 mins from putting the order in, if that. Driver has a weird vibe (motorbike helmet but he was driving a car?) says 'G'day mate' when he gives me the box. And it's like a cake box not a pizza box. Big one as well. I'm confused, think I might have the wrong driver or order but the receipt is stapled to the box. I open it at the kitchen table and am not really sure what it was meant to be. So basically, I think I'm looking at a cube of calzone (see pics). I get a bread knife to cut it, expecting loads of cheese or sauce and some spicy Chinese prawns and pork to come out or something but instead I just get noodles.

Like chow mein noodles spill out every where, and there's loads of little chicken balls and grated cheddar and bits of apple. I'm picking through this mess of noodles and I find a couple of raw tomatoes and bits of pepperoni, and Chinese beef plus two and a half boiled eggs. Dug to the centre of the cube and found a single pearl of mozzarella. Ate about half of it. Felt strangely compelled. Mistake. Dodgy stomach next day like having a hangover.

☆☆ – SHANICE IN BIRMINGHAM
ERRRR . . . .
Hawaiian pizza was like a poke bowl. not jokin pics below. tomato base, mozzarella (both hot) layer of cold sushi rice, then topped w raw salmon, avocado, apples (?) and edemame beans. did not attempt to eat sushi rice and salmon. seamed like food poisoning waiting to happen. got a full refund plus £20 as well? couldnt give them the money back for nothing so 2*s mostly for the free money lol.

☆ – REBECCA IN DURHAM
EVIL
evil vibes

☆ – GEORGE IN HULL
HAWAIIAN PIZZA COMES WITH APPLE INSTEAD
OF PINEAPPLE
I didn't even order a Hawaiian pizza.

☆ – BRIAN IN MILTON KEYNES, TOP REVIEWER
WOW! JUST WOW.

*Buckle up reader! This review is not going where
you think it is. Drawn in by Little Chitaly's amusing
portmanteau name and the very high rating score
(which has since been up and down more than a whores
drawers excuse my french) I convinced my very reluctant
ball and chain to order. We fill our basket with the
following:*

mapo tofu
chicken fried rice
king prawn chow mein
curry sauce
sticky pork ribs
prawn toast

*and, as we were feeling hungry and quite frankly very
stoned, we ordered a margarita pizza.*
*Now, highlighting the fact I have copped to being stoned,
every word I am about to write is true as I remember it.
I completed my order and, with a groan, realised I had
ordered from a restaurant purporting to be 86 miles away
from me. They accepted the order. I spent a moment
searching for my phone to cancel and was shocked to
hear our doorbell ring before I could finish typing the
number. 'No,' I thought. 'Absolutely not.' But I went to
the door and there was the driver, handing over my food*

and fleeing into the night with a quiet 'G'day mate' as he practically bounced off!

I begin to unpack/check the food as my wife hurriedly organises plates/cutlery. Thinking there must have been a mix up, I check the receipt stapled to the bag (see attached picture) – Little Chitaly, with our exact order, our address, etc.

I blame the weed and take the small drum of curry sauce from the bag. I open it, and instead of being met with deep gold and that pure umami smell – I get onion, tomato, masala spices. Reader, I am looking at a bhuna. And I chuckle, I think 'Well, did I really expect authenticity from Chitaly?'

But it got stranger. Our mapo tofu? A rich, red paneer tikka masala. Chicken fried rice? A pomegranate studded chicken biryani. The king prawn chow mein's closest equivalent was a king prawn butterfly, served with a neat pile of linguini. The ribs became a chicken shashlik, and the prawn toast? A samosa, of course. Our ill-advised pizza? A peshwari naan, ladies and gentlemen. I know they're not exactly definitive proof, but pictures are attached. It was actually a very good indian but what the fuck happened?

One star is mostly for mental anguish and distress caused. As an indian this was a solid 4/5, as a 'Chitalian'? Baffling.

☆ – ROB IN STOCKTON
WHICH MENU WERE YOU GUYS LOOKING AT?
Weird. When I looked at the menu it was limited – a small authentic menu, all shaanxi style cuisine and the menu was in mandarin and english. There were a couple of pizzas as well but didn't order them.

My mum's parents are from xi'an and I was excited to see dishes like biangbiang noodles and roujiamo on a menu in the UK outside of london. I ordered biangbiang nodles and roujiamo and what arrives to my door is 3 massive tubs of curry sauce taped to a pizza base.

I rang the restaurant and this guy with an Australian accent picks up. My Mandarin's not amazing but I tried speaking to him, and he was like 'you what mate nah no idea what youre saying don't know what that is sorry you have to speak english'. Bit surprised he didn't even seem to recognise mandarin when the menu had literally HAD mandarin on it. I explained what I'd been given was wrong and he said he had no idea what I was on about or what roujiamo was. When I asked if I was speaking to little chitaly he laughed and the call cut off really suddenly after this insanely loud static. Looking at reviews it seems no one else had the shaanxi-style menu. Must be an error with justeat some crossed wires somewhere – they paid me back no issue but this was still bizarre.

☆☆☆ – DAVE IN NEWCASTLE
WEIRD FOOD

weird food. wen i orderd i had 2 click n say i wanted bonelss pizza? pizza was stunnin tbh dough amazin soft source was best ever had cheese fkin lush but was covered in black pepper wen ordered pepperoni?? but so fckin lush orher wise i didnt mind. 3* just 4 weird pepper pizza. chinese food was LIFTIN man. bit into chickn ball and it was just batter thort itd just b that 1 but all of them just batter. sweet n sour sauce was vinegar w sugar and ketchup fckin ransid. fried rice was just noodles cut up really small w a hard boiled egg. must b italians?? They shudnt b doin chinese if they dont know wrf theyre doin just stick to makin absolutely mint pizzas man.

☆☆ – JACK IN GLASGOW
SPECIAL FRIED RICE SUSP AF

I got beef in black bean sauce flat mate got kung po chicken, got some starters (ribs etc) to share and special fried rice.most of the food was fine but we honestly just couldn't work out wtf meat was supposed to be in the special fried rice. Did not taste like chicken. Prawn shaped but not fishy. Porky but the texture was wrong. Had a mouthful made us both feel a bit sick so we left it. Also curry sauce was a bhuna or smth I think?

☆☆☆☆ – JAN IN DAGENHAM
GREAT FOR MIXED DIET HOUSEHOLDS

No problems like other people have mentioned (find it hard to believe we all ordered from the same restaurant sort it out google?). Have actually ordered from here twice before with no problems – enjoy Little Chitaly as my vegetariab 15 year old (who DOES NOT LIKE tofu and who can blame him lol) can struggle to find much he likes at a Chinese takeaway while it's everyone else's favourite. He said their pizzas are amazing, even if the toppings are a bit funny. EG: he ordered a Florentine pizza, and it was topped with a boiled egg rather than a baked one, and the vegetarian pizza he got the next time had quite a lot of garden peas on it. He said he didn't even mind as the pizza was so good.

Note about the driver though. Pulled up in a car but was wearing a motor cycle helmet. Came to the door, handed over the food, didn't say anything. We enjoyed our meal. We have a smart doorbell, camera is only active when there's someone there. He was stood there for about 20 mins, staring at the door, then he looked at the camera, then he left. Bit creepy. Not sure we'll be ordering again but see if I'm saying that the next time everyone wants a Chinese and SOMEONE wants a pizza XD

☆ – KELLY IN NEWCASTLE
NER MAN
*put apple on my hawaiin fucking minging coudnt get hold
of any one when i rang except for rude aussie c*nt then
justeat refused refund bc the didnt believe is so they can
suck my big clitaly* ♭♭

☆☆☆ – ANISH IN NEWCASTLE
I DON'T KNOW WHAT I EXPECTED
*I saw loads of reviews talking about them fucking up
the Hawaiian pizza and putting apple on it instead of
pineapple. I thought lol okay lets order one and see what
happens*
*Just came with pineapple and ham. It was fine! Honestly
a bit disappointing lmao.*

☆☆ – RINA IN CRYSTAL PALACE
*I ordered one off their pizzas (shudve read reviews lol)
bbq chicken and it was okay but there were chicken bones
on and throughout some slices really weird could've
choked honestly not too bad tho would try again if no
bones*

☆ – HANNAH IN CLITHEROE
DID IT AGAIN
*I ordered the special pizza again. I don't know why I did
it. Seemed more calzone like this time, in that there was
mozzarella and curry sauce (close enough) and it was*

mostly hot. Still a lot of noodles, but this time there was a shit load of prawn toast in the middle. Ate about half. Felt awful. Had to call in sick to work on Monday.

☆ – JEN IN BASINGSTOKE
JOKE VEGAN OPTION
BF ordered from here after his shift asked if I wanted anything, assumed there was nothing vegan and was gunna sort myself out for dinner but he said there was one. Looked at the menu just said 'vegan' nothing else. Was listed under 'meal boxes'. I thought fuck it go on then. Food comes and his is fine just normal Chinese think he got quarter duck and a chow mein or smth. Mine is in a paper box. He gives it to me and I think. Hmm. Cold and wet.
Opened it and it was a massive block of uncooked tofu. Not even pressed, absolutely soaking. Silken tofu not firm. Straight out the packet. Fuck off.

☆☆☆☆ – ANNA IN NORTHAMPTON
Just a really decent Chinese takeaway. Haven't tried one of the pizzas (lactose intolerant) but the vegetarian options are great. They do mapo tofu without pork mince which is really tasty, and spring rolls are top quality. Though a free bag of prawn crackers I got sent once was a bag of plain butter crackers and some crispy prawns. They were free and I can't eat them any way, but I was really confused. Always arrives extremely quickly.

☆ – HANNAH IN CLITHEROE
I DON'T KNOW WHAT MY PROBLEM IS
*I did it again. Not the cube this time, but half a crispy
duck (including spring onion, cucumber, pancakes, hoisin
etc) sandwiched between a margarita and meat feast. Ate
the whole thing this time. Felt okay but did not eat for 3
days afterward.*

☆☆ – LEO IN SCARBOROUGH
WRONG ORDER BUT VERY FAST REFUND
*Ordered quarter of a duck and some egg fried rice, and
got a joint of gammon with steamed rice and a boiled
egg. Refund was there before I messaged to ask what had
happened. Very strange.*

☆ – HANNAH IN CLITHEROE
TRIED TO FIND IT IRL
*After another encounter with the special pizza (this time
it was a folded over peshwari naan with some ham and
pineapple inside) I finally looked at the other reviews.
Seems like Little Chitaly doesn't have a fixed location.
May be a food truck or something. Tried to contact
justeat's website for their details and they wouldn't give
me any (at first) and I couldn't find it on companies
house. But THEN someone from justeat got in touch –
said they worked in comms and had been monitoring
the reviews here. Looked up the address and sent it over
as they were very curious and no one else at the office*

*seemed to find anything weird about Little Chitaly at all.
The address they gave me was just outside of London, so
drove there. Basically just a huge warehouse thing in a
retail park which was mostly furniture/DIY/carpet shops.
Door wasn't locked so I went in, maybe expecting some
kind of massive Chinese cash and carry or something.
It was like . . . a trendy Australian style brunch spot
in there. They had the menu on a black board and it
literally said 'A trendy Australian style brunch spot' on
it. No name though. All the staff (who were all pretty
white surfer looking girls with nice tans) looked at me
and smiled. It was busy but they all offered to seat me
in unison and I said no thank you, and left. And when
I left they said 'okay g'day' and I swear to god they said
'Hannah'.*

*When I closed the door behind me and went back to my
car, there was cake box on the hood. Could sense there
was a special pizza inside. Opened it and, yes, a special
pizza was there, a cube like the first two I had. Cracked it
open and there was just a single apple in it. Chilling.
Please DM me over at @Hannah_Special_pizza on insta if
you have any info. Am collating everything I know about
Little Chitaly there.*

Reply from Little Chitaly: ☺

Hollow Bones

Min found herself bound to a hospital bed, staring up at a patterned ceiling with a long, thick vein running through it. The vein pulsed, synced with her heartbeat – as if it were connected to her.

She tried to move her toes and couldn't, finding herself numb below the waist. Her fingertips prickled uncomfortably. She looked around. She was in a plain white room where the walls were melting, sometimes bleeding. Where was she? When was she?

She was six and sixteen and thirty-six. She was in school, at the night market, back on the ship. She was in Beijing, Tokyo and New York. She was on the CSS *Chengdu*, on Argo station. A searing pain, then nothing. Strange looming figures, tendrils of light, her life swirling around her. She was brushing the dirt from a bone. Over and over again, she was brushing wet dirt from a white bone.

She blinked. The ceiling was back.

'Hello?' she tried.

Hooting. Her translator was lagging badly – it caught up

a moment later, with a cheerful 'Hello!' mechanically piped into her ears. She let her head (which was heavy, and numb) loll to her left. Fen was there, sat by her bed. The sound of them breathing was the loudest thing in the room – air whistling in and out of their snub nose. Token Virrin – Ash had complained about their assignment to the ship. *Does every Co-op project need a token alien?* Earnest little linguist who stared too hard. Big bush-baby eyes.

'Where's my mother?' Min asked.

'Please, listen. There was a terrible accident, Min. Your translator was damaged. We were on celestial dwarf x256D. You were at an archaeological dig – the others were collecting soil and flora. I was on the *Chengdu*. You fell into a chasm. I don't know how. No one knows how. Do you understand?'

'I think so,' she said.

A brief hitch in the translation. '. . . dead. You were the sole survivor, Min. They came for you and they . . .' She couldn't make out the rest of the sentence. 'We were picked up by a Virrin transport – Central Government, not Co-op. We're on one of their vessels.' Fen performed an exaggerated shrug – their shoulders reached up to their furry cheeks. It had taken them a while to get the hang of it. Virrin shoulders didn't really *work* like that. 'I can't say I'm happy about it. I'm sure this is very confusing. There's a lot to catch up on. I've been told to use . . .' the translation cut out again '. . . keep it simple. That's hard, though. You know me. Wordy.'

'The *Chengdu*?'

'The Central Virrin Government have taken possession of the *Chengdu*.'

'You must be furious.' Fen hated the government, all governments. Fen would never need to vivisect for a soul, never need *proof* humans were people. 'I agree with you, you know. Full space anarchy is the only way to go.'

Fen lifted a furry finger to their mouth.

'We're on a CVG vessel right now, you know. The Co-op will send an envoy to collect us once you're well,' said Fen. Their mouth was completely out of sync with the translation – it was easier to concentrate if Min looked away from their face. Virrin were prey animals, nervous by nature – they found a lack of eye contact deeply unsettling.

'Sorry for not looking, hard to concentrate with the . . . lag is distracting,' Min said. She wanted to rub her eyes, but her hands were restrained. The lights were very low in the room, tinged pink. Soft. Fen did the smile they had worked on for hours in the mirror. It was not very reassuring (large fangs triggered an instinctual, animal fear) but Min appreciated the gesture. 'Struggling to speak, some. Fuzzy. Time is . . . strange.'

'Please, I understand.' Fen reached over, and patted Min's hand. 'They said I could unbuckle the restraints when you woke up, if you'd like. They said to tell you the dosage you were on has been reduced.'

'Who said? What am I on?' Min tried to move her head,

and struggled. Fen's fur seemed to flutter, like the wind blowing through dry grass. 'A dissociative?' It had to be. She was lucid in a flash, then bewildered, unstuck in time a moment later.

'The medics on this vessel have given you codamine,' Fen said, sheepishly. It was a very common Virrin painkiller but barely safe for humans. It was as addictive as an opioid, with dissociative, hallucinogenic qualities. If Min recalled correctly, it had some structural similarities to DMT. 'I'm sorry. It's typical CVG rubbish. If you're in Co-op space, your vessel *should* be stocked for both species. It's ridiculous. And illegal.'

'Illegal. You'll get arrested if you give me codamine.'

'It was an emergency. I'll see they get a fine for their poor supplies, I promise. The medics tell me they tried their very best. It's a very small dose, really, very small. Are you hallucinating?'

She nodded. Tried to explain the intermittent quality to her reality – her sense that she had become unmoored in time. But she could not articulate it. She mumbled and stammered in a way that made Fen tip their head in bewilderment. She gave up.

'Am I hurt?' she asked.

'Yes. Your legs. You broke them in the fall. You tried to run away from something, even though they were broken. You made it much worse than it had to be.'

She had been running away – she could hear the adult-sized bracelets jangling on her little wrists. She felt sick.

'It's because I stole from the night market. The shopkeeper saw me. It wasn't even my idea, it was Kiko's.' Kiko was always trying to make her do stuff like that. She went to pull at the bed sheet, and Fen took hold of her wrist. The pads of their palms were cool, and pleasant against her skin.

'I don't think so,' said Fen. 'Do you know what year it is?'

'It depends.' Min swallowed. 'Why are you holding my wrist like that?'

'Your suit tore at the thigh. Do you remember?' She didn't. 'Do you remember the mission?'

'Scouting for a colony. Visiting planets the Virrin visited hundreds of years ago and abandoned. I'm collecting arte-facts for the Co-op.'

'Thank you. There you go,' Fen said. They seemed relieved. 'So your suit sealed the rip, but there was a wound . . . It's . . . Something happened to it. We aren't sure what. I don't think looking at the wound would mesh well with the . . .' skip '. . . of the codamine. Loath as I am to say they're right – I agree with them. Please don't look at your leg.'

'They?' Min lowered her voice to a whisper. 'Did they abduct me?'

'They rescued us, Min. Doctor Nook is in charge of you. And there are a few nurses. This vessel is running some tests on bacteria on uninhabited planets. They happened to be looking at the same planet as us . . . which I'm trying not to look at as suspicious.' Fen sighed heavily. 'There are many . . .' skip '. . . here. They're doing their best to work out what could be wrong. If it's a bacteria, a parasite, something else. They verified it's not contagious,' Fen continued, their face positively undulating each time their mouth moved. They let go of Min's wrist, stroking her skin with their thumb. 'I'm sorry. Do you remember anything? Do you remember what happened to the others?' they asked very softly, like Mother asking about the bracelets: did you take these? Why did you do that? Explain why you did it, I won't be angry, I promise.

'The others? Where are they?' Min went to get out of bed, and Fen stopped her, pushing her gently back to the mattress.

Min had fallen into the canyon and called for help. Even at the time, she couldn't remember why she'd fallen. The rest of the crew had jetted down into the canyon to help Min – by then, she'd started screaming. Screaming, and screaming, and screaming. Then comms shut down. Fen (who was studying human languages, not empty planets) had stayed on the *Chengdu*. By the time they arrived, everyone was dead but Min, who was screaming away the last of her clean oxygen and bashing her helmet against the ground.

'Do you understand, Min? The others are dead, and the Co-op need to investigate. Ash, Kim, Jones and Shin. They're dead, and we don't know why,' said Fen.

This story did not ring any bells. She brought her hand, gingerly, to her face and wiped the tears she found there. This didn't seem real – how could it, while the walls around her jiggled? Fen's eyes seemed double the size she knew they were.

Ash was dead. Min had known Ash for the better part of a decade. They were both headhunted by the Co-op at the same time. Trained together. Jones was very, very young – this was her first job out of the military. Shin, she barely knew, a well-regarded biologist. Kim was an acquaintance, a xenobotanist. Min never emailed him back about poker night. She was up for it – she was just so crap at replying to her emails.

She'd have to make all new friends, now. Mother was going to make her go to Tokyo just to get away from Daddy, and she'd have to make all new friends. She couldn't even count past four in Japanese.

'This is all my fault,' she sobbed. 'It's so hard to remember all the numbers, Fen. You need to tell my mother how hard it is.'

'Please. No one is blaming you. No one said anything about numbers,' said Fen. 'You need to stay focused, Min. This is important. There are people coming from the Co-op in the next few days. They're looking at data from all your environmental suits for a full . . .' skip '. . . no one can work out why you left the dig site, and all of the footage from your bodycam is corrupt for the whole day. The audio is . . .' skip.

'I should call my mother,' Min said.

'Your mother is dead, Min. Don't you remember? It's been two years.'

Who was going to take her to her swimming lessons? She didn't even want to go.

Her eyes heavy, her head heavier, she swayed out of consciousness again and found Ash sitting on the end of the bed. He had a femur in his fist. He brushed dirt onto her sheets.

How many Skins do you think you're worth?
You said none and the hole said More.
You said one and the hole said Four.
Ichi! Ni! San! Shi!

★

A nightmare.

She heard hooting, barking. Gloved paws were grabbing her limbs. She was shuddering, spasming, uncontrollably spasming, every muscle clenching, cramping.

She tried to open her eyes and sit up but found herself restrained. She was tied at the ankles and wrists with something soft and thick. The light rang in her ears – she closed her eyes. Min grunted. She asked to have the lights turned down, but she didn't know who she was asking, or what language she'd spoken in, or if she'd even spoken.

Min tugged at her wrists again – no pain. She tried to kick her ankles and her jaw fell into a silent scream. Pain shot through her leg and her back – it was like she'd hit her funny bone, like every bone in the lower half of her body was funny, jangling with pins and needles and electric-shock sensations. It was dizzying – she opened her eyes again and the light rang through her skull.

She vomited. She sobbed.

The lights dropped, and a number of figures (blurry, but visible) surrounded her, hooting softly. One came close to her face – an environmental suit? A *hazmat* suit? Darkness again. She would not remember this.

★

Min regained consciousness. Impossible to tell how long she'd been out. Hours, days, months. Fen was still there. Different clothes, looking more or less the same, bickering with a second Virrin – nothing that her damaged translator could parse.

The second Virrin wore a coat buttoned to the neck and rubbery-looking gloves. They were older, their fur greying in patches, with more of a snout-like nose than the snub Fen had. Their eyes were dark yellow. Fen's were jade green.

Fen left the room suddenly. Min tensed, panicked, and the other Virrin looked at her.

'Glad to see you awake,' they said. 'I'm Nook. I am in charge of the medics here.' They nodded to the door Fen had just walked out of. 'Fen is very dedicated to you,' they said.

'We're close,' Min said. Hours spent together, Fen studying her smiling, laughing, crying, scowling, taking notes furiously. They watched movies, Fen studying the screen and Min in equal part. The ones they liked best were the ones that provoked extreme reactions – tears, terror, hysterical laughter.

'Please, if you could tell me, how are you feeling? Please, if you could let me know if you're struggling to understand me,' Nook said. They were holding a tablet, poking and typing while staring at Min.

'I don't want to be on codamine. Take me off the codamine. It's illegal, and you'll get arrested. You have to call my mother.'

'Please. We've been permitted. Emergency use. And, please, I would not recommend it.' Please, please, please. There's some preposition the Virrin had, some little noise to indicate delicacy, politeness, formality with strangers; Fen explained it once. It didn't normally come through the translator like this. 'You're injured very badly. If we were to take you off the codamine, the pain would be . . . exquisite.'

'But it's making it every year, do *you* understand? It's every year, and my mother is dead, but she *isn't*, and everyone is dead. And you just . . . You can't go backwards, but the codamine is making it backwards, do *you* understand? It can't be like this.'

'You're not making any sense. There are other . . .' skip '. . . we can give you to counteract the . . .' skip '. . . effects, if it . . .' skip '. . . but please listen and understand, that the risks may outweigh the benefits.'

'Can't you source anything else? Can't you see, can't you see what it's doing?'

Min gestured to the room, the way everything melted and wobbled and spun.

'I don't understand. I'm sorry.' Nook scratched their cheek. Skip '. . . from the Co-op will arrive in a few days. And when they arrive, they promised to bring more appropriate medication. You will, unfortunately, now go through the codamine withdrawal process. We will try to make that process as painless as possible.'

She felt as if the pillows were trying to swallow her head. Her mother told her this would happen if she smoked pot – it was a gateway drug. Even though everyone experiments at university, it was still a gateway drug. Even though it was legal practically everywhere. And now look at her. How could she do her Masters, her PhD with a codamine addiction?

'Do you think . . . I'll be fine to go to Columbia, after? The university, not the country. New York is back on the up after the war,' Min said.

'I don't understand you,' Nook replied. 'It seems you are delirious. Curious. Like your body has not acclimated at all to the drug. Though, it has only been three days,' they added. 'Please . . . listen. I'll begin the process of lowering your dosage tomorrow.' Min kept her eyes closed. Her face was still wet with tears. She was so exhausted. 'I am sorry, Doctor Wei. Please. You can sleep.'

★

A nightmare.

Fen at the end of her bed. Fen sucking the marrow from a broken bone. Fen crawling up her legs, resting on her thighs. Fen's leathery, padded hands pulling at the blanket and ripping her hospital gown. Their eyes flashing in the darkness, huge and strange, with their pupils blown out, black and fat.

★

She woke with her stomach churning – had she eaten? Had they fed her? Her gut twisted, stinging, acidic – as if she had begun to digest herself.

Time seemed still again. Min knew where she was. Why she was. CVG vessel. Injured. She remembered her thigh. There was a wound on her thigh so strange and ugly she'd been ordered not to look at it.

Just a peek, she decided. Just a peek.

She pulled back her sheet. The wound glowed softly.

She could not see the damage to the flesh clearly, but she could see a tear, about ten centimetres long, tapering at each end. Wide in the middle, and an eerie blue. It didn't even hurt. There were prickles around her joints where the breakages had been, but her thigh? Nothing. She touched the edges of the tear – it was velvet soft, with a little give – she slipped her fingers over the lip of it, and found it softer still, inside. It was pleasantly slick – not quite in the way she'd expect a wound to be.

She slipped her fingers inside, and felt no pain, only a

pleasant sensation of fullness. She did not feel hungry any more.

She felt something brush her fingertips. Not bone, or muscle, but something answering her touch – blunt and soft, not unlike a set of fingers. The other digits traced Min's fingers slowly, and ran down her palm, drawing small circles there, kissing the soft skin of her wrists. She shuddered and pushed her hand further inside the tear.

She felt lips brushing against the tips of her fingers, her knuckles. Moist, and sucking softly. The tear, and the muscles beneath it twinged, and drew Min's hand in further still, to the wrist, then to the elbow, till she felt she could reach around, touch herself inside, bring the kissing mouths and the digits with her. She squirmed. Her eyes rolled back into her head, and sleep engulfed her once more.

★

A memory, which felt like a nightmare.

The environmental suit's emergency alarm activated before Min knew what was happening. It was loud enough to drown out the sound of her bones cracking, the suit ripping, her body landing on the ground. Min had landed in a chasm – she couldn't remember the fall.

It was dark – the only light the dim glow of the environmental suit. Her gloved hands and padded elbows sank into the moist soil. She struggled, yanked her arms free with a pop and sat up on her knees. Pain, then a sharp prick at the back of her neck, followed by a numbness in her extremities. Her head was light, her panic fading.

'DISTRESS SIGNAL ACTIVATED. EMERGENCY ALARM ACTIVATED. PHYSICAL INJURIES DE-TECTED. BREACH DETECTED. YOU HAVE BEEN INJECTED WITH MORPHINE. PLEASE REMAIN STILL. CO_2 SCRUBBER COMPROMISED,' announced the suit. 'CO_2 LEVEL: SAFE. DO NOT ATTEMPT TO MOVE. EMERGENCY ALARM ACTIVATED. DIS-TRESS SIGNAL ACTIVATED.'

The suit's user interface flickered ominously on the inside of her helmet. Min attempted to ping the crew and was met with a static groan, a large red cross, more flickering.

'CSS *CHENGDU* OUT OF RANGE. PARTY MEMBERS OUT OF RANGE,' the suit warned. 'DO NOT ATTEMPT TO RECONVENE AT TRANSPORT. PLEASE FIRE A BEACON. DISTRESS SIGNAL ACTIVATED. EMERGENCY ALARM ACTIVATED.'

'I know,' she snapped. 'Stop the alarm.'

She pulled up the map – a bare-bones thing created from a cursory scan of the planet's surface. She was indeed out of range of her crew and the *Chengdu*, but she could see the transport: a lone, blue dot around two kilometres from her current position. Her dig site was marked on the map in green – it was almost directly above her. She looked up: a steep, jagged hill – too high to fall from without risking serious injury.

'What happened?' Min asked the suit.

'YOU FELL,' it replied.

'But how, how did I fall?'

'Y-Y-Y-YOU FELL,' it repeated.

★

She woke a few hours later to pain, and bloody, stinging fingers, and her sheets stuck to her wounded thigh. They were stained a dark rust red, and fused to the grooves of the wound.

She punched a call button. Nook arrived, bleary at first, then their face splitting into a bizarre fear-grin upon seeing the mess.

'Did you touch it?' they asked. 'Please – *why* would you touch it?'

She lifted the sheet. The wound had rapidly scabbed onto the sheet – pulling it felt like removing a layer of skin.

When were they going to call her mother? Nook sedated her. She dreamt of kisses, laughter in the darkness; her shipmates, her mother, her lovers. Her mother.

Mother would talk in numbers; Mother would live inside a telescope and hold the stars if she could. She found a new planet, once, and named it after Min – the moons for their cats; Mochi and Momo. Would they visit, one day?

Xenoarchaeology is a joke, said Mother, because she was a hard scientist. *The Virrin have their own archaeologists. They don't need a little girl who can't count to five*, Mother said, like Min couldn't count just *fine* in Mandarin. Like she didn't already speak English, too.

Mother showed her the flashcards. Each had a bone. Min had a bone in her fist, now, her tiny fist.

She looked to her leg. The whole thing turned inside out. She screamed.

Ah, a nightmare.

★

Her fingers had blistered. The tips had blistered where they'd gone into the wound.

Nook came, and frowned at her hand, as if it had done something to offend them. They popped the blisters (Min felt nothing) and analysed the fluid, huge eyes narrowed to slits. Nook dressed her hand themself and brought her lunch. They threatened to restrain her if she was caught touching it again.

Investigators from the Co-op had come and gone while she slept. They left her clothes, antibiotics, morphine, gel to synthesise appropriate food and naloxone, just in case. They trusted her care was adequate, and her injuries were easy to treat. But would they call her mother?

This was her first day back on solid food. They'd been spoon-feeding her nutrient drinks while she was half-conscious. Min, faced with a plate of food, found herself unable to commit to putting any of it in her mouth.

They had brought her a bread roll, an orange and a small cup of jelly. The bread roll looked like a ball of fat, and the orange like human skin; the jelly was red, a strange, jiggling cup of half-coagulated blood. Min stuck her thumb in the orange and peeled it. Though she knew the skin of the fruit was not *skin* and the juice running down her wrist was not really blood-red – her stomach still turned.

She threw the orange into a small wastebasket in the corner of the room. She tried the bread roll, but it became thick and cement-like in her dry mouth. She gagged, and spat a mouthful of wet bread back onto the small plastic plate.

Synthetic food. And low-quality stuff too, the kind with that cheap synth-gel aftertaste. It was prison food.

She pushed the call button, mashing it, and asked the nurse to take the rest of the food away, and just bring her a nutrient drink. The nurse obliged, and brought her a large plastic sippy cup. Min could see how blue the nutrient drink was – she sucked at it, finding the texture and flavour pleasant, like toothpaste.

Fen came to her soon after the drink did. Slowly, fur still fluttering in a breeze that wasn't there.

They complained about Nook while Min carefully sipped her drink. Fen and Nook had wildly differing political views. Fen all-in on the Co-op and Nook a loyalist to the CVG – which Min understood to be broadly isolationist, anti-human, regressive.

'Nook wouldn't even *entertain* the possibility of pre-industrial human abduction, you know. Even though we have *plenty* of evidence that the Virrin were abducting humans with abandon . . . and when I brought up post-contact abduction . . . you should have seen the way their teeth came out . . .' Fen sighed, and shook their head, stiffly, and for Min's benefit – as if she couldn't tell they disapproved. 'Absurd. I've said it before, and I'll say it again – if you didn't defect to the Co-op, you're probably a xenophobe.'

'We should leave when we can,' said Min. 'The food is terrible. Tastes of synthesiser. Did anyone call my mother?' Min still struggled with Fen's natural facial expressions – they looked uncomfortable, she thought, anyway. 'She's supposed to take me to the pool.'

'You could try our food,' said Fen. Virrin food mostly consisted of bitter fruits, live insects and raw meat. 'I'm sorry. It's probably not very edible for you, but . . . no synthesiser aftertaste. Maybe you could try the fruit.'

'My mother?'

'Min, she . . . she . . . um. We couldn't get hold of your mother . . . Do you remember where you are?' She did. 'So you know there are no pools on board?' She did, she supposed. 'What that codamine has done to you . . . The CVG have much to answer for with this vessel,' they said. 'I'm putting in a formal report as soon as we get back to Argo station. They *still* don't know what's wrong with your leg.'

She asked them who came from the Co-op – if it was anyone they knew, their project manager, or just investigators. Faceless investigators. She imagined suits in the room with no heads and they seemed to grow from the shadows. She closed her eyes and wished them away.

Fen said as much. Just suits.

'They seemed fidgety about the whole thing. I'm a little

worried. I even made them show their IDs because . . . I don't know. We should really get back to the Argo as soon as we can.'

Her dreams pestered her when her eyes were closed. She remembered the bone. The bone in her fist.

'Did . . . Did they find anything at the dig site?' Min realised the question might seem strange. 'Bones? Or . . . tech fragments, I don't know.'

'I'm sorry. They didn't say. Just that they were still scouting the planet, and the investigation was pending. Why? Have you remembered something?'

'I keep dreaming about bones,' said Min. 'Before I fell. I think I found bones. I can't count past four, but I think I found bones. The Co-op should check the dig site. That was probably what flagged on the initial scan.'

Fen blinked. Blinked rapidly. They were frightened. They did that when they were frightened. There weren't supposed to be any bones on that cold, celestial dwarf. There weren't supposed to be any bones.

'I have a contact email for one of the investigators who came today. I'll tell them to check the dig site ASAP, okay?' said Fen.

Min took a deep breath. Fen magnanimously pulled out their ComPad and began typing a message – their claws clicking against the screen.

'Wait,' she said. 'It's just a few dreams. Maybe they don't mean anything. I have a very active imagination for a girl of my age.'

'I know, Min,' they said. 'What's wrong with your hand? The bandages?'

'I can't remember.' Maybe she'd burnt it cooking.

★

More memories.

Min propped herself against the canyon wall and fired her distress beacon. A great, red firework, it hovered undulating above her position and pinged onto the map. The canyon, now illuminated, appeared bare aside from a few sponge-like growths escaping the rocks around her. Everything on this planet was spongy; from individual lumps of dirt to the mountains and canyons – all was soft and glittered wetly. She heard a damp gurgle somewhere in the distance – but there was too much morphine in Min's system for her to feel physically frightened.

Min focused on her breathing. She noticed a glow coming from a crack in the canyon wall – a sharp cyan against the deep red of the beacon. With each slow, steady breath, the light seemed to grow larger and brighter, till it left the crack in small, glistening tentacles. The wall of the canyon began to close in.

The light of her distress beacon began to fall away, a red curtain parted by strange, blue fingers of light emerging from the wall and creeping towards her. They swept over her feet, her knees and came to rest at her thigh. She felt like she was sinking.

There's a hole in its out-skin.

80

There was. A rip in her suit on the inside of her right thigh. The suit must have sealed off her leg already. The rip grew as the tendrils of light investigated the torn fabric and her thigh. She was bleeding.

And with so many tongues in its mouth. Did it ever learn to count past four? Ichi, ni, san, shi . . .

Many tongues in her mouth, but not that one. Min wracked her brain for the number five.

It's so frightened. How many Skins would it trade, though? Just to be away from this place? How many Skins?

Ichi, ni, san, shi . . . Min thought. Her eyes grew heavy.

★

When Min was alone, the wound called to her. The blisters on her fingers throbbed, and the flesh itself sang to her fingers, like a touch-starved lover. It seemed hungry, and empty, like a mouth with no stomach, or teeth.

She waited till Nook had clocked off, till the night nurse went on break. She undressed her hand, and inspected the blisters, finding they had split into fissures, narrow, but not entirely dissimilar to the wound inside her thigh.

She pulled back the sheets and tore through the dressing on her leg with a strength she had not expected to find. She slipped her fingers back inside and found comfort – as if she were holding her own hand, or stroking her own hair. Sinking her hands deeper into the wound, she waited for the ghostly hand to answer hers, for the tongues and the lips she may have dreamt the other night.

Fen burst into the room. Min yanked her fingers out of the wound, feeling like a teenager caught with her hands in her underwear. She hissed with the feeling of it and tugged the sheets back up around her waist. She sat up. Had Fen noticed? They seemed frantic, clutching a tablet to their chest. They had a bundle of fabric tucked under their armpit.

'Min. Min, I'm sorry to wake you,' they whispered.

They poked their head into the hallway, checking for medical staff, before locking the door.

Min could hear their breathing, and watched their eyes dart back and forth as they stabbed, panicked, at the tablet. They dumped the fabric at the end of Min's bed – a plain sweatsuit.

'The Co-op checked your dig site. I just got a message from the investigation team and they found . . . fragments of a bone. A human bone,' said Fen. 'No one from our party. Old. Diseased. They're coming to get us. An hour, they said – about ten minutes ago. Can you stand?'

'I don't know.' She'd been wearing a hospital gown, proportioned incorrectly on her body, tied loosely at the neck. She leant forward for the sweatshirt – it was the first time she'd moved in days and the room lurched inward. She gasped with the shock of it and as her lungs filled, the room expanded. She steadied herself and pulled her sweatshirt over her head and the hospital gown. She stank. She didn't remember them bathing her – and she hadn't been to the pool yet.

Gingerly, she swung her legs around (the room swung with her), put her feet on the ground and stood, trying her best not to labour the process. She remembered Bambi at the beginning of the movie when he hadn't learned to walk yet. She felt her fragile deer's legs unable to take her weight.

Worse than Bambi – suddenly much worse than Bambi. Her right leg, her wounded leg, gave out. Crunching like a breadstick, it audibly snapped beneath her, leaving her on the floor with her femur sticking out of her knee. She swallowed a scream. It didn't hurt – she felt an exaggerated version of the prickling she'd had in her hand – but the shock of seeing it was almost enough to make her vomit. She hoped what she had seen had been distorted by the codamine in her system but based on Fen's reaction, the way their lips had peeled back over their gums to reveal an eerie fear-grin, her mind had not exaggerated the injury.

Whatever Fen said became lost in translation. She heard only squeaking, and an error message echoing around the inside of her head. Fen rushed to her, skidding as they dropped to the floor, then pawed helplessly at her leg and matted their fur with her blood. It seemed thicker than it should be, darker, like she was bleeding treacle.

'Is it thick? Is the blood thick?' she asked.

'No, it seems . . . normal,' Fen said. 'It doesn't hurt?' She shook her head. 'They can't know that we're leaving . . . I . . . I'll get you a chair.' Min grabbed the sweatpants from the bed. She wondered if she could pull them over her mangled leg. 'Don't worry about those,' Fen said. They shook the blood from their paw, then did a double take – first glancing at the wound on her thigh, then staring. 'Did you pull off the dressing?' they asked. 'It's . . . What is that?'

'It glows,' she said. It was glowing now. Glowing blue and oozing a fluorescent liquid down her thigh.

'It's bleeding, not glowing.' Fen was sounding more and more exasperated with everything Min said. 'Did you . . . interfere with it?'

'It's hungry,' she said. Fen grabbed her wrist and looked at her fingers, now sporting miniature versions of the same fissures on the inside of her thigh. They were glowing, too – too small to feed, for now.

'Hungry?' Fen paused for a moment. 'Okay. Please. I'm just . . . I'm going to drag you to the dock.'

Min let them. They grabbed her beneath the armpits with their long-fingered, bloody hands. Fen dragged her slowly through the corridor of the Virrin vessel, pausing periodically to put Min down and pant; to scout ahead, check the maps placed through the hallways.

The hallways were so long – hotel hallways. She hoped they'd find the right room for the xenoarcheology conference. She was the keynote speaker.

'I'm going to be late,' Min said. 'What time is it?'

'Three a.m.'

'I'm speaking at one p.m. . . . Did I miss it?'

'No,' said Fen. 'You're almost there.'

The station intercom rang – Min's translator took a moment to catch up after the tone.

84

'DOCKING REQUESTED – CO-OPERATIVE VESSEL.
DOCKING REQUESTED – CO-OPERATIVE VESSEL.'

Fen's pocket lit up, and Min heard a faint buzzing. Fen was dragging her faster, their feet audibly patting against the floor, their breathing laboured.

Doctor Nook came around the corner, in sleepwear, baring their teeth with their fur standing on end. Min spotted them first – Fen did not, only noticing when Nook let out a harsh bark.

'Do not remove the patient,' Nook growled. Fen kept pulling her. Min hoped her talk would be busy – xeno-archeology was a relatively new field – Min hoped the scientific community could find value in her work. 'What happened to her leg?'

'Like a breadstick,' said Min.

'It's clearly more serious than we thought – she shouldn't leave,' Nook snarled. Their fangs were out, their snout was wrinkled.

'If you keep us against our will, the Co-op *will* consider that an act of war.'

'She's contagious.'

'You said she wasn't.'

'Not to *us*,' Nook replied. Fen began to drag her again, and Nook advanced – more predator than prey animal. Like the neighbour's dog that chased Min, once, when she was little. 'This happens every time we make contact with them, you know? They catch something. Then they wipe out great chunks of their population because they *don't*,'

Nook lunged for her, grabbed her by her left wrist and waved her cracked fingers, *'wash their hands.'* As if to prove a point, Nook grabbed her little finger, and yanked it. It snapped, completely, and hung from her hand by a thin piece of skin. 'You take her off this ship, she'll give it to half the Argo before it eats her alive.'

'We have no reason to believe you.'

'I'm sorry. You won't leave.'

Fen dropped her. She smacked her head against the tiles and heard bare feet slapping the floor around her – she heard growling, grunting and barking. She tried to lift her head, tried to stop her eyes from rolling back in her skull, and looked up to see the two Virrin locked in a violent embrace. They fought with their hands, pulling at each other's clothing and fur with their claws.

Min's neck gave out, and by the time she'd pulled her head back up, blood had been drawn, and was spattered across the corridor.

She was beginning to think she'd be late for the keynote speech after all. She looked up at the ceiling and lifted her wounded hand. She pulled off her little finger, and dropped it into her mouth – easy as ripping off a hangnail.

The skin of that finger was so thin, it fell apart like stewed meat and slid down her throat just as easily, gristle collapsing with a press of her tongue, and the bone crumbling between her teeth. She swallowed.

Fen had grabbed the doctor by their scalp – she saw them flex their claws, and drive them into Nook's skull.

There was a crunch. Fen squeezed, and Nook went limp.

So did Min. Dark again.

★

There was nothing else quite like the smell of the reconstituted air. Min was on the Argo. She opened her eyes – she was in her bedroom, and she was wearing her own pyjamas: an oversized T-shirt, covered in rabbits. Her vision was blurred, and her mouth was dry, with a foul taste that can only come from days without a real meal or thorough brushing.

Her stomach ached, empty and churning with bile. They had her hooked up to an IV, and a health monitor. She had those little stickers on her temples, and a needle in her right arm, which was bruised with several removals and re-insertions. Had they had trouble finding her vein? Or had she yanked it out in her sleep?

She went to touch them – the bruises – and found that her left arm now ended in a stump at the elbow, knotted with purple scar tissue. Her right leg, too, was gone, amputated at the hip. Relief. She felt only relief.

When she thought of the lights in the canyon, the voice in her head, she was glad the wound was gone – even if it had taken her leg with it.

Someone had left a glass of water, a nutrient drink and a catalogue of prosthetic limbs on her nightstand. There were crutches propped up against the mirror, by her bed – slightly out of arm's reach.

She grabbed the water with her remaining hand and drank it greedily, spilling it down her chin. She did the same with the nutrient drink, a glob of blue paste landing on her pyjamas.

She was no longer hallucinating – nor did she seem to be in withdrawal. She must have detoxed while she was asleep – an induced coma, perhaps, while they treated her.

A young man in scrubs entered her room, wielding a fresh catheter bag.

'Oh! You're up!' he said. 'How do you feel? Just to let you know, we had you in a coma while your body recovered from the surgery, and we got you all dried out from that alien shit you had in your system.'

'I've been better,' said Min. He introduced himself as Seojun, and checked her IV, apologising for the bruising around her arm. She had seized once or twice, apparently, during detox. 'How long was I out?'

'Ten days – but I've been here taking care of you. And Fen, too! They've been in your guest room. Um . . . sorry about your hand, and your leg, by the way? I hope it wasn't too much of a shock. You seem alright. Did you see the catalogues?' He trotted to the other side of her bed and dropped prosthetic catalogues (hands and legs in separate booklets) into what remained of Min's lap. 'We can get a new hand printed for you ASAP, once you pick a design. The leg will take a little longer – but by the end of the week, you'll be as good as new. Co-op's gunna cover it all and bill the CVG for it, so feel free to go nuts with the customisation options.'

She thumbed idly through the hand catalogue. It seemed she could pick almost any colour she wanted and choose from a selection of functional designs. There was a basic hand, which would work well enough, but there were hands for precision work, or for heavy lifting. You could even have a skin cloned from your own tissues.

'It was . . . just my left hand. I'm sure the basic one will be fine,' she said. 'But I'll think about the colour or maybe getting the skin . . . Can I brush my teeth? I assume I won't be able to walk unaided.'

'Probably not for a while, no. There's a chair in the den for you . . . I'll grab it, and your toothbrush. And Fen! I'll get Fen.'

Seojun sent in Fen and did not return – which Min was glad for. As pleasant as he seemed, Seojun was far too peppy for Min's mood. Fen smiled awkwardly – they had trimmed their claws down to the tips of their fingers.

'I'm glad you're up,' they said. 'How do you like your new translator! Brand-new design – with all my experimental coding, should be more naturalistic. Sorry to beta-test on you.'

It was funny. A good translator can trick you into *not noticing* the way your conversational partner's lips moved out of sync. The voice was different as well – less squeaky, coming through with a crisp accent – Fen sounded like a very fluent foreign speaker, rather than an alien with a poor dub.

'It's just nice to talk to you without a lag, again,' she

said. She noticed a faint, foul taste in her mouth – like an infected tooth. 'Or without hallucinating . . .' Min added. The two of them were quiet for a moment – Min didn't quite know what to say, how to ask. What the fuck happened? Did we start a war? Am I contagious?

Fen seemed to sense what was on her mind.

'Are you wondering about your . . . amputations?' they asked. Min nodded. 'You remember what Nook said? About the contagion? I chose to believe them when they said the Virrin were immune. After all, I'd been around you for days with no issues. When we boarded the transport – the Co-op had come with doctors, mostly Virrin, thankfully. I wouldn't leave the airlock and I told them about the nature of the infection. We did the amputation on the floor, with an all-Virrin surgical team. Does that make sense?' Fen asked. Not a flaw of the translation – Fen was nervous, panicked by the memory, sounding a little garbled.

'Am I cleared of the contagion? Do they know what it was?'

Fen cocked their head and perched on the end of her bed. They began to twiddle, idly, with a stuffed bear that had been placed at the foot of Min's bed. Not one she recognised – a gift, presumably.

'They isolated a parasite in your leg – just a . . .' the translation skipped, '. . . which is fairly common in the northern hemisphere of the home-world, living in the wound.'

'That didn't come through.'

Fen grabbed her tablet, and typed something in their native lettering. They showed her a photograph of a strange, ugly creature. A fat, blue slug. Min was not squeamish but she turned her eyes to the ceiling, and felt phantom hairs stand up on her missing leg.

'It had more or less hollowed the marrow from your leg bones and we found its eggs in your fingers. I think Nook probably knew about it right away and was letting it fester on purpose. I think they wanted to see how it would affect your behaviour – maybe to see how contagious it was. You only ever see it at a high altitude on the home-world, and they just don't burrow into Virrin,' said Fen. 'I think that's why Nook had you straight on codamine – they wanted to keep you confused. I . . . I don't know what it was doing on the celestial dwarf. No one does. Your dig site was a mass grave – all of the human bones showed signs of infestation. We think the parasite had been living on the planet for a long time. It seems that . . . Perhaps the Virrin brought infected human abductees there? Our best guess, anyway.'

That explanation only connected half the dots for her – everything else, the hunger, the voices, the lights. She'd have to write all of that shit off as hallucinations. They were just a product of the codamine. But the canyon, the voice and the lights in there – that wasn't so easy to write off. There was only a little morphine in her system when that light had spoken to her.

'What about the others?' she asked. Four people had died down there. There had to be something. Fen gave a stiff, guilty shrug.

'Not a clue. Their hearts stopped – no parasites, no tears in their suits, no equipment failures, no signs of a struggle, even,' they said. 'I know it doesn't seem right.'

'I think there's something down there, you know. Something . . .' Min struggled to find the word. 'Terrible.'

'Well . . . someone will look into it, I'm sure,' Fen said, sounding sceptical – as if she was still high as a kite and bleating on about swimming pools.

'I know what I saw,' she said.

★

She woke in the middle of the night with a foul taste in her mouth. Pain rang through her jaw, into her teeth, her gums and then her tongue.

Min stuck her fingers in her mouth, and felt for a crack in her teeth, a missing crown – she found nothing. Nothing but a ridge on her tongue, brushing her knuckles. She investigated it and found a soft split near enough to her uvula that she gagged when she touched it.

She went to pull her fingers from her mouth, but it called her back. It wanted her to run the tip of her finger over the lips of this split – it didn't care if that made her gag. Without removing her finger from her mouth, she dragged herself down the bed till she was across from the mirror.

She didn't even need to turn on a light; the inside of her mouth was lit with a soft, blue glow. A voice, not just ringing, not in her dreams, but clear as a bell.

Is it time you learned to count past four? How many Skins, this time?

She slid her finger into her tongue.

Goth GF

Willow from work is an adult goth and she's one of the most needlessly hostile people I've ever encountered. She thinks everything is shit – from the music we play, to the drinks we serve; to our colleagues' clothes and shoes. She's doing a PhD at my uni, but she won't tell me what it's about. She said, 'It's too complex for the undergraduate brain to comprehend.'

Everyone at work hates her except me. I think she's hot. She's so hot, she makes me want to throw up. She's so hot, that I googled 'does anything bad happen if you wank too much?' She's so hot that if she brought me a clump of that long, black hair of hers, pulled straight from the drain of her shower and asked me to eat it – I probably would.

I think she's the most beautiful woman I've ever seen in person. And her body is *nuts*. She wears these baggy metal-band shirts every day – but I can tell she's like *stacked* under there. She's casual, but less conservative on the bottom. Black denim short-shorts or this tight leather skirt. In summer she wears fishnets that bite into her thick thighs.

Pinching the flesh in a way that makes me feel like my eyes are popping out of my head and my tongue is rolling out of my mouth down to the floor and internally all I can hear is AWOOGA AWOOGA BARK BARK BARK BOYOYO-YOYOING.

And, I don't know much about make-up – but hers always looks really *really* good. It's obviously something she's really passionate about. I know that, because the 'tips' she's given to the other girls at work have caused some pretty big arguments.

There was the 'purple lipstick incident' – which happened back while Willow was still on probation. Clare came to work wearing purple lipstick. Willow asked her what brand it was. Clare told Willow the brand – and Willow said, 'Oh, so it's cheap.' First she told Clare she should've used lip liner, because it was 'bleeding everywhere already'. Willow then told Clare, 'If I were you – I'd avoid purple, anyway. It makes your teeth look yellow.' And launched into an (honestly pretty obnoxious) explanation about 'the colour wheel', which Clare recounted to me in infuriated detail the following day.

About a week later there was the 'colour match incident' – which I witnessed first hand. I was on shift with Willow and Carmen.

Willow said to Carmen (blunt not unkind), 'You have a line,' and pointed to her own jawline.

'What?'

'You have a line of foundation. It's too orange for your

skin. You should get a better colour match. Or at least try to blend it more.'

Carmen snapped back and said she didn't want to paint herself corpse-white, like Willow. And Willow laughed at her and said, 'At least my face matches my neck.' And Carmen stomped into the back room and cried next to the kegs.

I really didn't get why this was such a big deal. I stood at the end of the bar like a lemon, and looked at Willow, who threw her arms into the air like: *What's her problem?* Her jangly bracelets fell to her elbows, and for the first time I noticed the nasty self-harm scars on her wrists, and her forearms. Some of them were covered by a tattoo of an axe – others weren't.

Clare told Dave, the duty manager, that they shouldn't pass Willow's probation and he said, 'Fat chance,' and explained that Willow was the owner's friend's daughter. Our owner might even be Willow's godfather – Dave wasn't entirely sure. Clare made sure to tell everyone, complaining about the 'nepotism of it all'. She even called Willow a bully. And everyone loves Clare (who is bubbly, and cheerful, and is never hostile or negative) so everyone hates Willow.

In Willow's defence, Clare does almost always wear an unflattering shade of lipstick. It *is* often bleeding out onto her upper lip or smeared onto her chin – sometimes it travels up to her nose. Her teeth *do* often look yellow. And Carmen's face doesn't match her neck *at all*.

Our male members of staff thought the make-up stuff had been blown out of proportion and that Willow wasn't so bad – until she started commenting on their taste in music.

Dave put on Tame Impala one day and she said, 'Ugh, who put on this date-rapist music.' She called the Mountain Goats (my choice) 'whiny shit for wannabe wrist-slitters', and called Dan's beloved Billie Eilish 'Bibby Eyelash' and a 'fake-goth', and music for 'lame little TikTok girls'. When Dylan played the Arctic Monkeys, she turned them off and asked: 'What year is it?'

When it was asked that she play her own music – that she pick something – Dylan, Dan and Dave were all dismayed. She did not play 'sweaty music', as expected. No Korn, or Marilyn Manson, or Cradle of Filth to be found – Willow played only the most impeccably curated and obscure dark electronica and drone metal from foreign artists with wild and captivating backstories. She played the kind of music they pretended they liked but didn't really listen to.

But if that was not enough to breed a near universal dislike towards Willow (and it was), she also nags incessantly on shift. She'd nag me for pulling pints wrong, and for not tidying up when the bar was quiet. 'Time to lean, time to clean,' she says. Dave told her to stop berating me, but I said I didn't mind. She's older than me and she's worked at more bars; I just thought she was being helpful (if a bit sharp). Dave called me a pussy.

But I *really* don't mind. I prefer her feedback to Dave's. Dave's always really snidey about it. He lets you fuck up for months then pulls you to one side to have a massive go at you, like your foamy-headed pints were this huge character flaw. But he won't stop you from pouring a shit pint, nor will he show you how to pour one properly.

Willow tells me when I'm doing something wrong on the spot, so I can sort it out straight away. And she always says, 'That's better,' or 'Nice,' in her low, flat voice when I do it right. And then I bank the sound of her saying *nice*, and I think about it later while I'm furiously masturbating to the memory of her teaching me how to clean the beer lines or make a decent pisco sour.

The other men hate being nagged or corrected by her. They call her a patronising cunt. I've started thinking of them as *sex-idiots*, because only someone utterly deficient in the realm of erotic intelligence could fail to understand Willow's immense appeal.

Shortly after she passed probation, we all went out for 'work drinks'. When she didn't turn up, they called her a bitch and started whingeing about her – went on about her for hours. They ran out of reasonable stuff to pick on, got drunker and nastier, till Carmen started going for her self-harm scars.

'She thinks those bracelets cover them up, but they just draw more attention,' Carmen said. 'That's probably deliberate, though. Attention seeker. Probably fucking borderline or something.'

'Is borderline the one that makes you a massive fucking cunt?' Dave asked.

'Come on,' I said. 'That's not on.'

Dylan said I was being a snowflake, and they all laughed at me. Then they started looking for her on social media – they hoped to find a post that could be a 'firing offence'. Dan found Willow's Instagram quickly. He found her quickly because she has fifteen *thousand* followers.

I don't use Instagram at all. I have an account, but had deleted the app from my phone before I'd even started uni. I felt like an idiot for not looking her up before.

There was a lot of bland stuff; gothy clothing and make-up reviews – pictures of her with friends. Tattoos, piercings. Then there was the risqué stuff. Sexy selfies – sex-toy reviews. Pole-dancing videos – she is an experienced hobbyist. Dave showed us a picture of her hanging upside down from a pole, anchored by her right thigh as her left foot was stretched out towards the ceiling. I thought about the vast amounts of money I would pay to put my head between her legs.

Someone in the comments once called her reviews *Harsh but fair*.

Dan read aloud a post about overcoming self-harm and called her *Cringe*. They all screamed at a picture of her holding a little black vibrator she'd been sent by some eco-friendly sex-toy company to test. Part of the review said: *This is perfect for teasing. I'd love to tie someone down and torture them with it.*

I left the drinks. I told them I wasn't really comfortable laughing at someone's posts about self-harm – and they did what people tend to do when they know they're in the wrong like that. They doubled down. Took the piss out of me. Acted like *I* was in the wrong.

Later Clare and Carmen texted me privately to say they were sorry, and things did go too far.

I didn't see those texts till the morning. I spent the night furiously masturbating over Willow's Instagram after I redownloaded the app. At one point, I accidentally knocked my knuckles against the 'follow' button. I panicked and unfollowed her. Then I realised that would look weird – that she'd probably still get the notification. So I followed her again. Then I unfollowed her. Then I followed her again. Then I unfollowed her. Then I followed her again. Then I fell asleep.

I had a dream about working behind the bar with her. I was completely naked, and she was fully clothed, and she was calling me a moron while I poured pints with too much head.

The next shift we worked together, she asked me to unfollow her. I was just relieved she didn't notice the multiple *follow* and *unfollows*.

'I like to keep this stuff separate,' she told me. 'I know it's a bit cringe, but I just like getting free stuff. I don't like people at work knowing.' She was wearing a baggy Sunn O))) shirt, black shorts and black tights. 'I'm going to remove you as a follower, anyway. I just wanted to let you know.'

I told Willow I sincerely thought her Instagram was cool, and she snorted at me. She said: 'Sure you do,' and spat on me, a little, by mistake. And I decided I wanted her to spit on me properly. And then I went bright red and went to the bathroom to calm down.

I kept thinking about the picture she posted of the snake tattoo wound around her left breast. She said in the caption she'd never pretend tattoos aren't painful, but she loved 'the place' the pain put her in. I didn't have any tattoos, so I didn't know what she meant, or what 'the place' was.

When I was ready, I came out of the toilet and tried to talk to her about her tattoos. 'Do they mean anything?' I asked. Couldn't get much out of her. She said:

'Not everything is deep, dude. I just think they're cool.'

I emailed a tattoo artist while I was on break, and two Saturdays later, a guy called Robin with a shaved head and a massive beard was tattooing a snake to my right forearm. And it was intense. I sweated the whole way through and shook when it was done. It felt like a bad sunburn and I liked that. It reminded me of being little and being on holiday; of childhood summers spent baking outdoors, and stinging, red skin.

When I took the cling film off the tattoo and washed away the plasma and blood, I imagined Willow slapping the tender skin. And then I wanked off with my left hand, because my right arm was sore and I didn't want to get jizz on the tattoo by accident.

I got the tattoo a week before our work party on Easter

Saturday. We all went out for a meal and I intentionally sat next to Willow. She noticed the fresh tattoo, and said it was 'cool' even if snakes were a little overdone. She asked which shop I'd gotten it done at. I was elated. *I did it to impress you*, I almost told her.

So I told her which shop, and we chatted about the artist who did it. She told me Robin had tattooed her chest – which, of course, I knew. Because I found Robin via her Instagram.

'It's so itchy,' I said. 'The artist tried to sell me some tattoo butter, but it was a bit pricey on top of the er . . . the ink.' And she gave me this *tiny* little smile. She told me not to waste money on *tattoo butter*.

'Just get Bepanthen,' she said. 'It's nappy-rash cream. Same stuff and it's much cheaper.'

I imagined her rubbing the cream into my tattoo, her cold, pale fingers slick, and pressing on my skin.

During the meal, Willow was so mean to Dylan that I was jealous. He asked her if she had ever heard of *Pulp Fiction*.

'Seriously? Are you fucking twelve or something?' she snorted. And I memorised the way she said it – and later, I imagined she had ground the toe of her boot into my cock, and I prematurely ejaculated, and she asked me: *Are you fucking twelve or something?* She then asked Dylan if he'd heard of *Jurassic Park*.

At the cocktail bar we moved to, I asked Willow to tell me more about her tattoos, 'Because I really want to get more now.' While she told me about all twelve of the tattoos she currently has, she showed most of them to me, even pulling down the collar of her shirt to show me the head of the snake on her breast.

I told her I think her tattoos are hot. She said, 'Okay,' rolling her eyes at me, and left to get a drink. I folded my hands over my crotch in an ecstasy of embarrassment. I hoped the lighting would disguise how red my face was. Willow barely spoke to me for hours. Instead, she argued about Tame Impala with Dave. She grinned at him while she tore into his taste in music, downing espresso martini after espresso martini.

I stared at them. Clare had a go at me for being miles away, then asked if I was single. Later, she trailed a hand up the inside of my thigh, in full view of everyone. I saw Willow looking at us, and I hopped up, and went outside to smoke. I don't smoke. Everyone knew I didn't smoke. I left Clare cringing at our booth and stood outside with my face in my hands.

'That was brutal,' said Willow. She handed me a cigarette. 'But she is way too old for you.' I put it in my mouth and she leant over, and lit it for me.

'She's only twenty-five. You're about twenty-five, aren't you?'

'Twenty-eight.'

'Well, I don't think you're too old for me.' I coughed around the cigarette. She smirked at me. Her lipstick was dark red, curling into a little Glasgow smile at the corners of her mouth – a print of the rim of her martini glass. She looked me up and down.

'No thanks,' she said. And that *was* brutal. And the worse she made me feel, the more I wanted her. I smoked more of the cigarette, trying to build myself up to saying something. I was torn between denying I liked her like that and begging her to reconsider. But I couldn't speak – because my throat was tight, and my eyes were filling with tears. 'Oh my God. Don't be such a baby.'

I wiped my eyes on my sleeve.

'Sorry,' I said.

'What are you, nineteen?' she asked, in the same tone she asked Dylan if he was twelve.

'Twenty,' I said. And she told me her last boyfriend was thirty-two, and she thought *he* was immature. 'You wouldn't have to date me,' I told her. 'I'd do *anything* you wanted me to. I'd let you do anything.'

Her eyebrows shot up. They are jet black; plucked and pencilled into a judgemental arch, designed to make you wince when weaponised against you.

'Oh my God,' she said again, and called an Uber – which she clarified was *just* for her. She put out her cigarette and told me this conversation had absolutely exhausted her; she told me to say bye to everyone for her. 'Let's never talk about this again.'

I smoked the cigarette to the filter; she shook her head at me as she got in the taxi. She looked like she felt extremely sorry for me. I wanted to lick her shoes.

I went back into the bar and told everyone Willow had left – Dave complained she'd just gotten fun. Clare patted the space next to her, sheepishly, and I told them I was going to head off as well. Clare seized up again, too drunk to hide her embarrassment.

'Oh no, don't go,' she said, the *because of me* implicit.

'Don't worry about it, I'm just knackered.'

I went home and had a sad wank over Willow's Instagram.

After the Easter party, Clare had her shifts rearranged so she wouldn't be on with me, and Willow had a week off for uni.

Dave told me he didn't get why I didn't just let Clare feel me up. He explained that Clare was 'actually quite fit'. She once got changed into her gym gear in the bathroom before her shift finished, and she had a really nice body. Yes, she was a bit plain, but Dave would rather go out with a bird with a fit body and a plain face, than a pretty bird with a shit body.

I told Dave I just didn't fancy her. Dave asked me to rank the girls by fitness. I said no, but then he called me a snow-flake again, so I said Willow, Carmen, then Clare. Dave snorted, and said the correct order was obviously Carmen, Clare then Willow. I said Willow was really pretty. Dave said he didn't go for that goth shit. 'Maybe if she scraped the corpse paint off.'

He also said he hated 'Instagram girls'. I'd started following him when I reactivated my account, and his page was full of pictures of his trainers, and mirror selfies captioned like #MensFashion #CheckMyFit #RateMyFit #OOTD #StreetStyle #Men #Muscles #BartendersOfInstagram or whatever other needy hashtags he could pile in. I pointed that out to Dave – that he was on Insta all the time. And he said, 'Not like an Instagram girl, though.' I said girls are normally a bit more self-aware.

'Tell you what,' said Dave. 'You like *Willow* so much, you can be on every shift with her. See how much you like her after getting nagged and ripped to shreds every shift.'

Joke's on you, I thought, *I love being nagged.*

I hadn't seen Willow since I told her I'd let her *do any-thing* to me. When the new rota was posted, I basically shat bricks. I thought Dave had been joking. But no, he'd set out the rota so I'd be working alone with her three weeknight shifts back-to-back. And the bar was fucking *dead* on week-nights – after nine, ten p.m., it would just be the two of us.

On the Tuesday, it was incredibly awkward. We literally stood there in silence for an hour when we had customers in. Willow made excuses to go and check the kegs. Then she decided to inventory the spirits – an especially boring task which Dave had been putting off for weeks.

I stayed on the bar all night. Then we cleaned with our headphones on. She didn't even nag me. At home, I searched 'goth girl' on Pornhub and scrolled till I found an actress with the same haircut as Willow. But the girl in the video was submissive, and I didn't like that. So I tried 'goth dominatrix' then 'mean dom goth girl' then 'mean dom goth girl destroys twink' and those all worked – but 'mean dom goth girl makes twink cry at work and spits on him because he can't pour a pint to save his life' was too specific a search term.

On Wednesday, I broke the silence. The bar was empty, so I told her I was sorry for being weird. Her hair was covering her AirPods. She pulled them out and asked if I said something.

'I said I was sorry. For being weird at the party.'

'Yeah, you were pretty drunk, I guess.'

I was about to argue with her, when I realised she was giving me an out. I could say, *Yeah, I do say some shit when I get that drunk; I always get so emotional and weird.* Or I could tell her I hadn't had that much to drink, that I'm obsessed with her, and the meaner she is to me, the worse it gets.

'I wasn't. Not really.'

'I'm not going out with you,' she said. 'I don't go out with boys who are younger than me. I just don't. You don't seem very mature, sorry.'

'I don't want to go out with you,' I said. She rolled her eyes.

'Well I'm not going to have sex with you, or whatever. Be your work fuck buddy, whatever the fuck you were angling for,' she said. But she didn't say that she *wasn't* attracted to me, which I decided was a good sign. She was brutally honest, and I think if she had zero interest in me, she would've just said I wasn't her type.

And the thing is, I know that I actually am kind of a

baby version of her type, because I looked all the way through her Instagram, and I saw her boyfriends and her girlfriends. And I saw broad, masculine men with big beards and pretty faces. And I saw gangly, masculine women, with lots of tattoos and pretty faces. They were all much taller than Willow.

I am something between broad and gangly, and I have a pretty face. I will probably fill out in my mid-twenties. I am much taller than Willow. I do not have a beard, but neither did the girlfriends.

'I don't want that,' I replied. She looked sceptical and stood in silence for a moment.

'Sure,' she said. Lip curled, eyebrows fully weaponised. I looked at her, pleadingly. I hoped she was connecting the dots. I always imagined she would be able to, because of her posting on Instagram about vibrators and tying people up and stuff. We stood in a long, painful silence. She sneered at me.

'I like it when you're mean to me,' I explained. 'I want you to bully me.'

She narrowed her eyes.

'What the fuck?' she said. 'You total fucking freak.' I turned bright red. 'This whole time you've been getting off on working with me? You're a . . . fucking disgusting little man,' she said. I could feel my eyes welling up, and I could feel my cock getting hard. Willow dropped her outraged demeanour suddenly. In a flat voice, she asked: 'So that? You want that?'

I did want that. I do want that.

And we agreed I would give her all of my tip money for the foreseeable. We agreed she would treat me like complete dirt at every given opportunity. We agree that's what I deserve. We agree that I am a disgusting little man.

Extinction Event

1

We found the Objects on a desert planet. Cold deserts at the poles, hot deserts at the equator. Though the word desert feels like an understatement. At its hottest points, water would boil away as easily as the chlorine that choked the air. At the extreme poles, that chlorine froze into eerie stretches of piss-coloured ice. Too hostile to sustain any life but theirs.

We found them all over the planet, the air around them so clean and fresh you could pull off your helmet and breathe were it not for the punishing temperatures. Rooted to the ground, their arms flower and reach to the sky; they respond to stimuli and lean together for comfort. At once flora and fauna – neither or both – but a lifeline either way. If they could drink in chlorine and pump out oxygen – the potential to repair Earth's ruined atmosphere seemed huge.

We dug up five of them, half a tonne of alien dirt, and flew them back to Lazarus Base.

No one from the space exploration department knew what to do with them. Xenobotany did not exist as a field of study then. It was decided they most resembled cacti and I was made their guardian, because I study cacti.

But they are not cacti. Cacti do not cringe from your hands; they do not shiver and shake. Those first five were brought to me in a state. They looked like they'd been shoved in the back of a moving truck. They were battered and bruised, and they flinched and writhed when the guards and I potted them. They were like nothing I had seen before. A dry spine snapped from one of Subject Three's arms, and what trickled from the hole was neither sap nor blood; thick, and syrupy, and a deep, dark red.

I decided to name them individually. Didn't like calling them the Objects; I felt that to be hostile designation. Their planters were labelled one, two, three, four and five. I named them Una, Deuce, Trinity, Ivy (like, IV) and Quinn.

The other botanists came to look at them – tried to diagnose them, fit them into a taxonomy we could understand. An expert in sea plants wondered if they might be better understood as some kind of echinoderm – something more akin to a starfish than a plant. I sent a formal request to base management and asked for a specialist in starfish from Oceanic Preservation to help me. I was told to worry about harvesting their seeds; that I would not need an echinodermologist to see if these *things* could grow in Earth's soil. So I carried on.

I took care of my charges as if they were cacti, and this seemed to be enough for a time. They perked up. Their clay-coloured epidermis took on a healthier, greener tinge. I suspect that this is not necessarily the *correct* way to take care of them; that they are just remarkably hardy. I accidentally spilt a coffee on Una once, and it wiggled happily, and took on an even healthier, greener colour.

I was allowed to refrain from harvesting their seeds until their bruises healed. Though the director of Botanical Studies took care to remind me that we are on borrowed time as a species.

Our apocalypse should've come years ago. It was delayed by back-to-back pandemics, mass protests, pedestrianisation, banning of fossil fuels and finally 'terrorist' attacks on Fortune 500 companies. Shortly before I was brought to Lazarus Base, the BP bombings dominated the news – a mass destruction of their buildings, their pipelines, their executive branch (the head of the snake). I remember telling my partner, perhaps coldly, *One man's terrorist*, with a cheerful shrug. And he smirked back at me, his white teeth peeking from between his lips.

A week later, I was bundled into the back of a van. One moment, I was in a research outpost in the Atacama desert, the next I woke up here. I was with a handful of other scientists who'd been working in the Americas – the third batch of kidnappings in as many weeks. We found ourselves among the best and brightest minds in climate-related sciences from the world over. All of us dragged from the street, our offices and our beds to Lazarus Base – where human ingenuity would *solve* the climate crisis.

Management (we do not know who brought us here) hung a clock in the cafeteria – ticking down by the second, the time we had before the planet was truly unsalvageable. When I first saw it, the time read: *5 years, 201 days, 11 hours, 32 minutes, 40 seconds*, then *39 seconds. 38. 37. 36.*

According to the Clock, I had been here for around a year before the Objects were brought to us. I hope my partner (my parents, my friends) know where I am; they've all surely assumed. They talk about Project Lazarus on the news, but the coverage makes the whole thing seem a lot more voluntary than it was. Is. We have no internet access, but I imagine organisations set up by our loved ones; *Bring our children, parents, siblings and lovers back from Lazarus Base.*

Would I leave? The work is so important. But we are frightened. Some of us are hopeful, some of us give way to despair – at the mercy of that ticking clock. A woman from Microplastics hung herself with three knotted-together white jumpsuits. They're only letting Microplastics have one suit at a time now.

*

At first, I struggled to find their seeds. They were flowering, but their flowers seem more like plumage, more decorative than functional. I was reluctant to take samples.

I remembered the way Trinity shuddered when its spine was knocked off.

I went to speak to the director of Botanical Studies again (name unknown to us, just Director Viridi, to match the jumpsuit). I told her again that I would benefit from some input from an echinodermologist. The more I looked at them, the less they seemed like plants.

Viridi didn't like the idea. Wanted me to get on with it – involving other departments could be a waste of time.

'Get it done. Just get it done. If this all goes well, we'll name it after you. *The Babalola Tree*. Do you like the sound of that?'

'They're not trees,' I told her.

'I don't know if Oceanic Preservation can spare any staff when this whole thing might be a dud,' she admitted. Many wonder why we bother to mess around with the strange life forms that the space exploration team keep bringing back to earth. Would they not be better used in a search for a new home for us? Why clean up our mess when we could simply leave it behind. 'Is there anything easy I can do? Any equipment I can get you?'

My request for a set of hand-held biometric scanners was quickly fulfilled. I found them awkward to scan myself and drafted in Ji-Ah to help. Ji-Ah is part of the team who have been tasked with finding the source and the cure to the fungal disease that is ripping through what is left of the Amazon.

Our friendship was created by the proximity of our labs and is very reliant on the spotty universal translators we have clipped to our jumpsuits, hanging awkwardly around our necks, stuffed into our pockets.

Ji-Ah took one scanner, and I took the other. Arms stretched above my head, I could comfortably reach the top of the Objects, but Ji-Ah needed a step stool. We began at the top, and gradually moved the scanners down over Deuce (currently, the most robust of the Objects). The scan, showing on my computer, revealed something like an egg-sack, and a cloaca. I asked Ji-Ah if she knew if starfish have egg-sacks. After a moment of waiting for her translator to process *egg-sack* in English and spit it back out in Korean, she shrugged, frustrated on my behalf, and said: 'The hell if I know.'

Their flowers contain stamen, which retract back into their flesh like an animal's penis. The cloaca is near the root. The scan revealed no teeth or spines, but I was a tad concerned about acids, or other defence mechanisms they may have.

No brain, but a central nervous system. Something like a circulatory system. Too difficult to tell without dissecting one. I noted down my findings, but I didn't flag them. I was worried I'd be told to cut one open and I couldn't imagine vivisecting one. I was increasingly sure that they could feel pain and I was at a loss.

I let Ji-Ah go, and pulled on a thick glove, coated with a corrosive- and heat-resistant gel, and I crouched by Trinity's planter. I extracted an egg, one half the size of my palm, which reminded me of a passion fruit seed; a dark-coloured pip, wrapped in a sturdy, red jelly.

I brought the egg/seed over and up to the most easily

accessible flower on Ivy's arm. I was taken aback when the flower seemed to detect the presence of the seed/egg, and its feather-petals closed gently around it. Ivy leant in to me, accepting the seed, like a well-trained animal slowly closing its mouth around a treat.

I extracted another egg/seed, from Ivy's planter this time, and placed it on the rim of Quinn's pot. I watched as Quinn bent, its trunk suddenly as flexible and elegant as a swan's neck. Its feather-petals closed around the egg and it stood tall once again, back into its usual place.

'Remarkable,' I said aloud to no one. I did this again, with Una's egg, and Deuce's flower, and I filmed it. While I sent the footage to the director, there was a dramatic puff of pollen from Trinity. The pollen looked like heavy, red snowflakes. And from the flower fell a pulsing black pellet. I quickly snapped on a gas mask and deposited the seed in a nearby planter. I filmed the dramatic ejaculations of Ivy and Una, and collected a sample of their pollen. I left the room, switching the ventilator on, light-headed and elated, three new planters pregnant with new life.

Those new Objects grew in days. I named them the Earthlings. The air became so pure in the facility that we switched off all the filters. We didn't need them any more.

2

I keep the five original Objects, and the first three I fertil-
ised. I grow another handful and they are sent in pods of
five to test in polluted places; from China's great industrial
cities, to the ruins of London, to the blackened, uninhabit-
able counties of California, to Chernobyl and the
Fukushima power plant. We try them in oceans, rivers, in
the Arctic. They thrive. And they *clean.*

After positive, unexpected results in the Arctic,
Microplastics commandeer one of my Earthlings – one
I had named Septimus. It shivers when the guards take
it away. Apparently, the test batch appear to have been
cleaning the oceans, quite literally removing micro-
scopic particles of plastic and converting them to fresh
air. They want to test this in a controlled environment,
to make sure their field results weren't a fluke. They
don't tell me when they'll be bringing Septimus back.
But they tell me that the Objects do appear to clean out
microplastics. In fact, they seem to swallow anything,
from plastic bags and sanitary pads, to chemical and
nuclear waste.

I am called into Director Viridi's office. She shakes
with excitement. I am told that I will have to breed thousands of them. I will breed thousands of them, and they
will be deployed all over the planet. Vacuum cleaners for
our collective garbage, they will cleanse the plastics from
the oceans, and the CO_2 from the atmosphere, and

temperatures will drop and so will sea levels. The director looks mad. I think she might cry.

I am given a team and an orchard. Then, when I am too careful and too slow, they take the orchard and the team away from me. Some jackboot agrarian expert is pulled in to supervise instead, and I'm sent back to my lab, to continue to assess and monitor 'the test group'.

★

At dinner, one evening, I fret to Ji-Ah. I complain that they took Septimus weeks ago, gave me no estimated time of return, and no one at Microplastics will respond to my messages.

'You gave them names?' she says. Then she tells me to keep my voice down. That I should just be patient. That nothing bad will happen. 'They're too valuable,' she says.

Then we watch someone from Biodiversity (red jumpsuit) climb onto a dinner table.

'Why won't they let us call home?' he asks. 'My mother lives alone, all on her own. If we all, if we all,' he waves his arms, urging us to stand, 'if we all *refused* to *tolerate* these conditions, then they couldn't—' A guard tasers him in the leg. He collapses, and the guards drag him out of the room. We all go back to our food.

Septimus is returned to me the following morning by a pair of sour-faced guards. The others seem to perk up when it returns. Their colouring brightens, they stand taller, firmer. I am in the habit of chattering to them now, and I say: 'Septimus is back, aren't we all pleased to see it?' like a schoolteacher, welcoming a pupil back from a brief illness. And I think they agree with me. They jiggle in place, and the air feels fresh.

The fruits of my stolen orchard, meanwhile, have been dropped all over the world. The news we watch at dinner talks about the miraculous 'Lazarus Tree' which will save us all. (I am not sore about the name – though I do think Babalola Tree had a better ring to it.)

Wherever Lazarus Base is (the middle of an ocean; none of us are sure which) we pick up Indian news channels. A beautiful news anchor calls them *an all-natural super-charged Roomba* and grins, with huge white teeth. Channel changed – now a Chinese news anchor groomed within an inch of his life says: *I hope you weren't looking forward to a hot one this summer, because global temperatures are set to plummet thanks to the work at—* Channel changed again. A kids' show about talking monkeys. The episode is about flood safety. That stays on.

★

I go to the lab around a week later and find Septimus quaking in its planter. It sits between Juno and Octavia. Septimus has three arms. Two are stiff, bolt upright, the third swings violently. This is the most I have seen any of them move. Its epidermis is unhealthy and chalky-looking. It seems drier, spinier. Its feather-petals lie scattered on the dirt, it is flowerless.

I am chilled. I approach, cautious, aware that something

has gone horribly wrong. I cannot stop Septimus from moving, but as I approach, it stills, shivering with the offending arm outstretched; a leper reaching for Christ. A sort of mould has formed, near the join between the arm and the trunk. It is gooey, and green, and at the centre of the mould seems to be a small, white head. I change into a hazmat suit. I prod at the white head with a cotton swab – it erupts. Not a head, but a fat orb of *pus*, now dribbling onto the ground. Septimus shakes more violently, wrenching its arm back and forth, back and forth, till I am forced to back away. I bag up the cotton swab and decontaminate. I run for the director's office, because I do not know who else to tell.

'Something has gone wrong,' I tell her. I had to pound on her door for five minutes before she would let me in. 'One of them, they're sick.'

'One of the original trees?' she asks.

'No. An Earthling,' I say. She raises her eyebrow at *Earthling*. 'One of the ones I bred, I mean. Grew. Number Seven. The one they sent to Microplastics, for tests.'

Begrudgingly, the director tears herself away from her paperwork and plods along behind me, sceptical when I suggest she decontaminate and wear a hazmat suit.

By the time she suits up and we are back in the lab, Septimus has almost ripped off the infected arm. Twisting, limp now the arm is partially torn, that thick, gelatinous sap/blood has sprayed itself on the floor, on the wall, onto Octavia. I throw a cup of water on Octavia, to rinse the blood/sap away, and it shudders, huffily.

'What on *earth*, am I looking at?' asks the director.

I cut off the arm. I use the largest, sharpest sheers I can find. Septimus is rattling and shaking in the planter, until it once again detects my presence. It goes still and allows me to remove the infected appendage. I chop carefully; I do it in one, hard clip. When the arm hits the dirt, it shudders.

The rot is deep. That white pus and green fuzz is deep into the tissue, gloopy, and messy, and reminding me of a rotten vegetable, forgotten at the back of a refrigerator.

I ask the director to fetch Ji-Ah. She does not return – Ji-Ah entering the room in the director's hazmat suit. After barely a cursory glance at Septimus and my samples, she tells me this is not a fungal disease. Nor does it look like any ordinary bacterial disease one might see in a plant, or a tree, or vegetation of any sort.

Together we look at the severed arm, and we find veins, and multiple layers of dermas and nerve endings, which all look animal in nature.

'You need someone . . . someone who isn't a plant person,' Ji-Ah says, shaking her head. 'This looks like the black plague.'

I am told not to go back in the lab once Ji-Ah is finished. With a flourish, the director tells me the severed arm will be 'sent away for analysis'. And that is that. I am locked out for the rest of the evening.

★

I have a nightmare. At lunch, we are all served rotten vege-
tables, and I am the only one who seems to notice. They all
eat, happily, and I gag. They ignore me when I tell them to
stop eating.

The following morning, they bring me the echinodermologist – petite, bespectacled and white, they are
practically frogmarched into my quarters, barely giving me
time to dress. They are Australian, with an oddly sickly
countenance; not like the tanned, toothy Australians I had
seen in hotels and waiting tables back in Lagos. They intro-
duce themselves as Doctor Isla Robinson, and look shiftily
over their shoulder at the guards. They are like a prey
animal, hunched, nervous. I am tall, I loom over them.
I extend my hand and catch one of the guards shaking his
head from the corner of my eye. I curl my palm inward.
Robinson looks as if they have been dragged here, rumpled
with their blue jumpsuit inside out.

'Ayoka,' I say. I try to inject it with a little warmth.
'People call me Ayo . . .' They are glaring, both of them,
behind us. 'Or . . . Doctor Babalola is fine.'

They don't like us socialising on the clock.

The first month we were here, I saw a man I recognised
from the university of Lagos teasing a guard. They were both
Indian, both with SHARMA stitched into their jumpsuits.
And the Sharma I knew kept asking guard Sharma, 'Come
on, where are you from? Maybe we're related,' sniggering; as
I understand, *Sharma* is a very common surname, and it was
clearly a stupid question. 'We could be distant cousins,' he'd

said. 'What's your mother's name?' And guard Sharma had clubbed my Sharma over the back of the head with a baton. My Sharma, a tenured professor at one of the world's best universities, was on the floor, drooling blood. One of the world's leading minds in meteorology, clubbed so casually.

None of us tried the guards, after that. Though I did hear a rumour that someone on the space exploration team got tasered a few days later.

'Let's see this latest last, best hope for humanity, then,' Robinson says, dryly.

'I've been asking for someone like you for ages,' I tell them. 'Even just to come for a look. They told me no.'

'Come on,' urge the guards. They accompany us to my lab, and watch carefully as we suit up and go through decontamination. When the door closes behind us, Robinson shakes their head at me.

'They seem a little more . . . full-on, today,' I say.

'I'm on suicide watch,' they reply.

'Oh,' is all I can manage. The overwhelming sense of urgency and despair among the thousands of us here, goes largely unspoken. It is jarring to have it acknowledged.

They tell me they aren't allowed to use sharps unsupervised; the guards check in every twenty minutes, and clearly resent that they're spending so much time on Robinson.

We enter the lab and find Septimus thrashing wildly in its planter, rotting from the tip down, pus sliding down the trunk, flopping back and forth from the middle. The rot from the severed arm has spread. Next to it, Octavia has developed a clump of pustules right by the root, and is quivering, like a tiny dog at a vet's office.

'Good God,' says Robinson. They circle the Objects, flinching when Septimus moves, shuffling to the healthy plants, where Robinson seems to oscillate between terror and wonder. 'This looks like . . . There's this wasting disease that has decimated the sea star population . . . I . . . My research is largely about getting around this disease, preventing it and promoting breeding. They. They pull their own arms off, and they just . . . rot. They rot if you don't catch it early enough.' Robinson looks at me.

'But it's treatable?'

'A strong dose of antibiotics will work early on, in a starfish but . . . Christ, what even are these?'

I share my findings. For hours they pore over my material, with the guards popping in and out. Robinson concludes they should've been involved from the start; aside from reproduction and their ability to synthesise, they're far closer to an echinoderm than a cactus.

'I asked for you. I really did,' I say. 'Someone who studies sea plants said—'

'I wouldn't worry too much. I suppose I'd have been guessing, too. The aesthetic similarities, the way they feed and process stuff, that's . . . planty. I mean you don't *plant* a starfish so . . .' Robinson's glasses fog inside their hazmat suit. 'Neither of us really knows what we're doing. And these are out in the world, now?'

'By the thousand.'

★

We load Octavia up with antibiotics and hope for the best. But Robinson tells me that Septimus is probably too far gone. I ask them if they think the Objects can feel pain. Septimus doesn't have a brain, does it? So it isn't suffering.

'Starfish feel pain,' they say. 'Or, at least they sense it. Without a brain, it's hard to know if they do or don't *feel*. You have to remember, these things aren't even from planet Earth. That nervous system of theirs could well serve as a brain. They could have some kind of consciousness we don't understand,' they tell me, gravely. 'Or they might not.'

'Let's hope not,' I say. But I don't quite believe it. 'Sometimes, I think they understand me. I feel like they respond to their names, and they . . . react when I'm there.' I try to demonstrate. I say Ivy's name, and wait for it to respond, in some way.

Robinson looks at me like I'm insane.

It takes Septimus two days to fully disintegrate to a pile of gooey, white mush. I'd wanted to uproot it, to put it out of its abstract misery. But we decided not to touch it, keep it contained to its planter. We isolated the others, had them taken out to the orchard, while we watched Octavia.

The antibiotics work.

And then they don't.

The outer pustules disappear, but then Octavia stops moving completely – over the course of a few days, it goes a funny, pale shade and gradually collapses in the middle, into a pile of white rot.

Octavia had contact with Septimus, and Septimus had contact with Microplastics. The conclusion seems pretty cut and dry, to me. The others seem to mourn them. They droop, and sag, and take less food. Trinity, particularly, begins to shudder ominously when we discuss the disease.

Before long, I get a report that the disease is popping up all over the world. In China, twenty are wiped out in a week, and then in Antarctica, the same. Iran, America, Chernobyl. They waste.

But they clean.

Air quality jumps and remains stable. The water around them is truly clean; plastic-free. Temperatures drop by .05 of a degree, worldwide.

*

We study my remaining six, Robinson and I. 'My' team continues to fertilise, and breed, and ship them out to their deaths.

I come to the director with our findings. We tell her that they are not trees. We tell her that they are in pain.

'I think it would be ethical to suspend the use of the—'

'The Lazarus Tree,' said the director.

'The Lazarus Tree . . . We really should stop calling them trees . . .' I trail off. 'I think we should suspend their use, until we work out how to prevent the wasting issue.'

'Why?'

'Because . . . They're in pain. I think they're *distressed*—'

'Distressed?' She snorts at me.

'Yes. The others . . . *sag* when there's a death, they *shake*. I think they're afraid. And we're hurting them. On purpose. If we know they're in pain it just seems wr—'

'Wrong?' The director rolls her eyes. 'Babalola. They're *working*. They're working better, and faster than anything we've tried. Any research, any solution. We plucked them out of the sky, and they're *working*.'

'But . . . How are you disposing of them? We don't even know if this is communicable to humans, or other creatures or—'

'They're working.'

And that was that.

They take me and Robinson off the project. I am back to cacti, back to my action plan for the preservation of desert plants. Back to my desk. I do not see or hear from Robinson again. My emails to them bounce.

We are allowed limited access to broadcast news and they continue talk about *the Lazarus Tree*. The wondrous alien plant discovered by the intrepid space explorers of Project Lazarus, studied and bred and thriving with the help of botanists at Lazarus Base. Our Death Clock has ticked up two whole years.

At dinner, we watch a Nigerian news report – I recognise the broadcaster and the anchor. She is taken out on a boat to the Gulf of Guinea to see one of the West African pods *cleaning out our oceans and potentially saving the world.*

She pauses on her boat to explain the benefits of the Lazarus Tree in front of the nearest pod. While the reporter speaks, cheerfully, I see Una trembling over her shoulder. I see it wrenching its arm back and forth. I see white spots on the trunk.

Nightstalkers

'I worry you'll regret it,' said Mom.

'You dropped out of high school, too,' Keith replied. 'You're fine.' They were stacking shelves together. Mom was the assistant manager of the store. They were making her 'oversee' the canned-foods section – some idiot had shelved a bunch of expired beans a couple of weeks ago and now no one could be trusted to stack a shelf unsupervised.

'I didn't drop out for fun,' Mom reminded him, inspecting the expiration date on a can of beans. 'I got pregnant. And I always thought that was a cautionary tale, not a piece of advice.' She paused and plucked the red uniform vest Keith wore over his shirt. Her vest was blue. 'A couple of years ago, it was all *I'm not gunna end up like you, Mom, I'm gunna get out of Santa Carla*,' she said. Keith winced, embarrassed by his casual cruelty.

'Yeah well . . .' Keith mumbled – he checked the base of a can (not expired) then slammed it on the shelf harder than he'd meant to. 'I suck at school. At least they pay me to be here. Santa Carla's not so bad. I like the beach. I like my friends.'

'And when your friends go to college next year?' she asked.

'Tommy isn't going to college.' Mom made a face. Either she was disappointed, or she'd found a can of expired beans. She didn't like Tommy, even though he'd been Keith's best friend for years – she said Tommy was spoilt and rude to his mother.

'Tommy's still in high school, at least,' she said.

'Only 'cause his parents are making him,' he said. Keith nudged her. 'If I'm not in school, it gives us time to focus on our music,' he told her. Then she smiled.

'Sure would hate to deny the world of the musical stylings of Si-son and Gar-mom-kel,' she said. The joke name of the band they pretended they were starting. Mom was teaching Keith to play guitar. Mom used to perform at little bars all over southern California before Grandma died. Dad had been out of the picture for a long time already – she had to give it up to take care of Keith. She didn't talk about it often – he figured she didn't want to make him feel guilty. He felt guilty anyway. 'Did Tommy find a bassist yet?' she asked. Keith shook his head.

'We need a singer, too,' he said.

'You can sing,' Mom said. Keith shook his head. The idea of singing in front of Tommy made his skin crawl.

'We were thinking of getting a girl.' It was Tommy, fresh out of work at the record store – a summer job for

him, way cooler than a supermarket. Tommy had promised to speak to his manager; ask if Keith could take over
his job once he was back to school. 'Like Patti Smith
but . . . way hotter,' he clarified. Mom smiled at him, her
face tight.

'I think Patti Smith is very pretty,' she said. Tommy
snorted.

'Can I take him for a smoke break?' Tommy asked,
slinging an arm over Keith's shoulder. They were the same
height. Tommy had been taller till early last year. Mom told
Keith to be back in ten minutes.

They went out back by the dumpsters; Tommy gave
Keith a cigarette.

'You get Lucy?' he asked. He tossed his hair – light
brown, shot with sunshine blond. He was growing it out.
His tan had darkened to its summer shade, and his skin
was busy with freckles. Tommy swallowed – and Keith
watched his Adam's apple bob in his throat.

'Huh?'

'Acid, you got any acid?'

'Oh. Sure,' said Keith. Tommy grinned – his dad was a
dentist. He had these big, white California teeth.

'I got this *real* hot piece coming to the beach tonight.'
Tommy lit his own cigarette, had Keith lean in close to
light his. He always made Keith come to him, would never
just give him the lighter.

'Your mom's friend's daughter, right?' Keith asked.
Tommy had mentioned it a few times last week. *If I have to*

babysit a tourist, she'd better be hot, he'd said. 'Is she our age?' Tommy nodded.

'Her name's Rainbow,' he said, smirking. Keith took a long drag of his cigarette. 'But we call her Rain.'

'*Rainbow*,' Keith said, lip curled.

'I know. Her mom was a hippy for like five minutes before she got knocked up and went back to Minnesota. Rain's got the stupidest accent. So fucking cute.' Tommy smiled as he spoke. 'She's real excited to drop acid.'

'Sure she can handle it?'

'Probably. Give her half a tab, see how she likes it.'

'Fine. But if she freaks out she's your responsibility.' Keith reminded Tommy of the pair of tourists Tommy had brought to one of their little beach parties about a month ago. Keith had gotten stuck babysitting one girl on a bad trip for hours while Tommy fucked the other in the back of his car.

'Won't happen again, man. I owe you one,' he said.

Tommy offered to pick him up from his apartment, give him a ride to the beach even though Keith usually walked. Probably wanted to make sure Keith didn't forget the acid – Keith had 'forgotten' to bring it once or twice before when Tommy had threatened him with the presence of a random girl. Nothing fucked up a trip for Keith more than a stranger freaking out. Made him anxious. Made him angry. Made him resent Tommy.

★

At home, Keith showered, then changed into the Pink Floyd shirt Tommy had swiped for him a few weeks back. It was tight – maybe a girl's shirt – but Tommy said it looked good on him. They'd stolen it from a clothesline in Playa Dorada, the fancy neighbourhood in town.

Tommy lived just outside Playa Dorada, but acted like the people there were some class above him. A privileged upper class, so naive and sheltered that they left their clothes out all night, failed to lock their doors or hide their valuables.

They act like they're in Bel Air and not fucking Santa Carla, Tommy had said, as they cut through the cul-de-sac to get to Tommy's house. *Except they're too good for LA. Heard one of the Stepford wives tell my mom the city's too scary. Like this town isn't just as bad. Idiots don't even lock their doors.*

He'd pushed open the porch of a pretty lilac house to prove his point. Then he walked in. Crossed the threshold, turned back to Keith, grinning and crooking his finger for Keith to follow.

And Keith did. He'd always been more of a follower than a leader.

The first couple of times they did it, they just looked around. Looked at the pictures hanging on the walls, laughed at their records, revelled in the taboo of hanging out in someone else's house. Keith liked to sit on their couches, see what was in the fridge. Keith and his mom lived in this little apartment; a lot of their stuff was inherited from Grandma, so it was all a little raggedy and mismatched. Some of the rich-people houses had all-matching living rooms. Huge couches, and loveseats and recliners, all the same shapes and fabrics. They were like dolls' houses. He imagined living in a house like this – imagined the space. Imagined the money.

It was easy to take a little petty cash. Take fifteen, twenty dollars left carelessly on the counter from these people who already had so much. They wouldn't even miss it.

While Tommy escalated to stealing jewellery and silver-ware, Keith stuck to cash. Too much of a pussy to take anything that might be missed.

Soon, they were breaking in to houses every week. Tommy just wanted to take stuff – and Keith could no longer linger in the homes the way he once had. In and out in a few minutes, with a handful of dollar bills he'd use to buy comic books or soda or weed.

Tommy never tried to get his girls in on it – Keith liked that. It was their thing. Their secret. He hoped they'd do it tonight – that Tommy would ditch *Rainbow* and they'd head to Playa Dorada high off their asses to see what they could find.

Keith wrote a note for his mom – *Back late, maybe staying at Tommys, see you in the mornin!* – stuck it to the fridge, and waited around for Tommy. He stuck a six-pack in his backpack and stuffed a soft pack of cigarettes into his pocket, a mix of menthols and pre-rolled joints. He extracted a sheet of blotter paper from its hiding place – between the pages of an H. P. Lovecraft story collection. He smirked at the blotter art – a line drawing of a naked old man with a long beard – a speech bubble above his head read *One square . . . and you're there!* Keith tore off a band of tabs – stripping the old man of his cartoon feet. Five in total – one for Keith, one for Tommy, one for *Rainbow* and a little extra, just in case.

Tommy showed up later than he said he would, with the girl in the back of his car. She was their age, but she *seemed* younger. A wide-eyed tourist – sunburnt, and very blonde, her eyebrows a streak of white across her red face. Her hair was long and ratty with saltwater. Keith decided, in that moment, he preferred brunettes. Mexican or Italian girls, with tanned skin, and bold eyebrows and thick, black eyelashes you could actually see.

She was wearing shorts, and this ugly, beaded poncho thing. Keith couldn't tell what the poncho was covering, maybe a bikini top. She was red and white and wispy – Keith didn't see what was appealing about her.

'Hey,' she said. 'Rain.' Keith grunted his name as he climbed into the back of the car.

'Tell Keith about Charlie Manson,' said Tommy. Rain launched into this dumb story about her mom meeting him once before he was a psycho. She sounded like she was from Bumfuck Nowhere – accent thick and provincial, practically mooing out her Os. She turned back to Keith, blinking at him, her eyes violently blue in her bright-red face.

'How come you're in California?' asked Keith, guessing she expected him to make conversation. She grinned.

'My mom's getting divorced. Stepdad, not my dad. She wants to move here!' She seemed so excited. 'So we're touring the state, picking a new place to live. Isn't that awesome? Do you love it here?'

'I guess,' said Keith.

'I'm so into the sunshine. I'm gunna have such an amazing tan once this peels,' Rain said. 'I'd love to live here.'

'Cool,' said Keith. He leant forward and turned on the radio. Their local station was playing Hendrix.

'Urgh,' said Rain. 'So old.' Then she fiddled with the dial till she got to a station playing 'More, More, More'. Keith leant forward to change the radio back but Tommy slapped his hand away.

'You fucking hate disco,' Keith reminded him.

'This song's not so bad. It's kinda sexy,' Tommy said. Keith felt like Tommy had slapped him in the face. Keith had expressed a mild enjoyment of *some* disco *once* earlier in the year, and Tommy had called him 'a disco cocksucker' for weeks for it.

Fuck this, he thought. *Fuck him*. Rain began to sing along. *Fuck her, too*.

Keith pulled the tabs out from his wallet and dropped one on his tongue.

'Is that it?' asked Rain. 'Can I have some?' Keith deferred to Tommy. Tommy made Rain promise not to be a baby, made her promise not to tell their moms if she freaked out. When Rain argued that her mom wouldn't mind . . .

'Well mine fuckin' would, so . . .' That was that. Keith split the tab in half for her with a little pair of scissors he kept in his backpack.

'You can ask me for the other half in three hours. That's the earliest I'll give it,' Keith told her. Rain rolled her eyes and took the tiny scrap of paper from him. She let it sit on her tongue, pulled down the overhead mirror to watch the little rectangle swell with saliva and slowly disintegrate till she finally swallowed.

★

Their private corner of the beach was guarded by rough, dangerous rock. Only locals bothered to clamber over it – it freaked tourists out. Rain seemed unsteady and thrilled by the sight of the small, empty beach; the come-up seemed to hit her like a truck the moment her toes touched the sand.

They started a small bonfire even though the sun was still up. Keith started to giggle and Rain started to giggle with him, and she didn't seem so annoying to him any more. A fellow traveller, with him on the trip while Tommy lagged an hour behind, still more or less sober.

Rain kept running her hand close to the fire, so Keith picked her up, and dragged her a few feet away from it while she giggled and wriggled. Tommy shot over to them and started bitching to Keith.

'She's mine,' he said.

'She's not a fucking toy, Tommy,' said Keith, who had been raised on what Tommy called 'that bra-burning shit' and had little patience for Tommy when he was being an asshole like this. Keith so preferred Tommy on his own, so loathed the person he became when girls were around. Single-minded, aggressive, territorial – like a starving dog with a juicy steak.

'You still can't fuck her,' Tommy said.

Rain wasn't listening, rolling in the sand and shrieking with laughter. She turned onto her belly and traced her fingers through the sand. She went quiet, drooling a little as she stared at the shifting sand.

'I don't wanna,' said Keith. 'She's red, white and blue. I like Spanish girls.'

'Spanish girls?'

'Yeah.' Keith sniggered. 'Spanish girls. With a bunch of black bush hair.'

Tommy laughed, howled, tipping his head back. Here was the Tommy that Keith loved. Laughing, carefree, not territorial, or weird. His hair was brown, and shiny, and glowed in the firelight. His skin was the colour of caramel, sprayed with freckles. Keith thought about dragging his tongue up Tommy's throat, cringed, then couldn't shake the thought. Tommy's freckles melted and reshuffled into flowers on his neck.

Tommy was in hysterics. He kept repeating the words *bush hair*, over and over again. Keith fell into the sand with Rain, while Tommy splashed in the sea.

'Disco cocksucker,' Tommy said. Or at least, Keith thought he said *disco cocksucker*. But Tommy was far away, down the other end of the beach, picking up driftwood. Rain had begun to crawl towards him, leaving Keith on his own.

Just the drugs talking. Chill, he thought. He heard the words echo around his skull, in different voices. Whispers and shouts; a chorus.

He made shapes with his fingers in the sand. Love hearts, faces, dicks and naked women, he surrounded himself with protective glyphs, drew a circle in the sand. He watched the patterns dance, melt, snap back to place whenever he blinked. When he looked up, Tommy and Rain were rolling in the sand together, their bodies tangled, melding with each other. Then they disappeared together.

Keith drank a couple of beers on the beach alone and watched the sunset. His high at its peak, the sky on fire, cotton-candy clouds swirling, curling, melting into a vast, lavender sea.

He started to cry. He wasn't sure if it was the drugs, or the sunset, or Tommy. Tommy. He thought about kissing Tommy on the lips. Tommy's tongue in his mouth. Tommy's teeth on his neck. Truths arrived to him comfortably with LSD, and those easy revelations would retreat like the tide as sobriety returned to him.

Fuck this, he thought. He paced the beach, collecting his scattered things. His lighter. He picked it up, then forgot he'd picked it up, then looked for it. Then he looked for his cigarettes, which were in his pocket. Then he forgot he'd found his lighter already. He lost his backpack while it was on him and spun on the spot, patting himself down for his lighter, looking for the backpack he was wearing. He looked around – paranoid he was being watched. But they were long gone and he was all alone.

Climbing over the rocks back to the main beach was a struggle. He was convinced he would die for a moment, that he'd fall and snap his ankle, and be swallowed up by the sea.

'Keith?' He thought he heard Tommy's voice. 'Keith!' Again. Just the drugs. He didn't even bother to turn around.

It felt like it took hours but he did get off the rocks, off the beach, and onto an empty sidewalk. It must have been late.

He walked to Playa Dorada in his flip-flops and took them off when he got there. Smooth roads, manicured lawns. He liked the feeling of the moist grass between his toes.

He looked at the houses, and wondered if he could go into one on his own. With Tommy it was fun – like a prank. Alone, he'd be just another peeping Tom; a creep and a thief.

Sometimes he and Tommy would see them. Other shadowy figures ducked into a rosebush, peering into the ground-floor bedrooms of these cute, single-storey houses. Tonight, Keith thought he saw a peeping Tom around every corner. Every rosebush seemed to morph into a dangerous, wild-eyed guy, crouched and masturbating furiously, making eye contact with Keith as he strolled, barefoot through the nice neighbourhood. All the porch lights were off, and he walked deeper into the little suburb than he usually did, down one of the cul-de-sacs.

He sang quietly to himself, a Carpenters song his mom liked. Tommy caught him listening to a tape of 'Close to You' once and had mocked him mercilessly. *Karen Carpenter has a three-octave vocal range*, he thought to himself. *Three-octave vocal range.*

He came to a house that was pink. He could tell it was pink, even in the darkness. Pink with a white roof. During the daytime, it'd look like a cake. He could taste sugar, and his mouth felt prickly. He shuffled to the back of the house and tested the door there. Open. Popped open with a welcoming sigh. *Hello, Keith*, said the house. *Hello.*

The back door led straight into the kitchen, which smelt freshly painted. The smell of it almost stung, stripped his nostrils; it was extra acrid, more paint-stripper than paint. He drank straight from the tap of a glittering, newly installed sink. The most beautiful sink Keith had ever seen. He ran his hands over the lovely white countertops. He shuffled to the fridge, a pastel pink. Again, he could just *tell* it was pink, like this cake-frosting house, but glossy this time, like candy. If he licked the fridge, it'd taste like artificial strawberries, or cherries. But he wouldn't. He wouldn't lick the fridge, because he was not that high.

'Pretty fucking high, though,' he said aloud. 'I am pretty fucking high.' And he giggled to himself.

Keith, the house whispered. *Fucking idiot!*

Keith spun around. Tommy. There was Tommy. Not a hallucination, but Tommy in the flesh.

'Oh,' he said.

'I've been following you forever,' Tommy whispered. 'Why'd you run off?'

Keith shrugged. The room was jagged now, harsh, closing in around him, heart pounding, chest aching.

'You wanted me to wait on the beach for you? Like a fucking dog?' Keith asked.

'Don't be mad. You're freaking me out,' Tommy snapped – he dragged Keith outside. They stood on the lawn for a moment, then ran back out into the street when the sprinklers clicked on. Tommy lit a joint, took a long drag and passed it to Keith – who accepted it.

'Where's Rain?' Keith whispered. He took a deep drag of the joint. They sat on the sidewalk, smoking in silence. The clouds above, which had been settling, were now crashing around above him, and the sidewalk shimmered like an ocean. Ocean above, Ocean below, Ocean to the west. He could hear it. If he really, really focused, he could hear the ocean.

'Left her in the car,' Tommy said. 'We were getting hot and heavy, then she starts laughing. Says my face looks stupid when it's close to hers and she was laughing so much she was shaking like a bug. Made me think about when you try to kill a cockroach with a can of hairspray. Got grossed out – didn't wanna fuck her any more.'

'So you came to find me? Figured maybe I could suck your dick instead?' Keith said. Tommy put his hand over Keith's mouth.

'Gross,' said Tommy. He didn't move his hand away. He looked sad, and serious. His palm felt hot on Keith's lips.

'I don't think we've been in that house before,' Tommy said. He squashed out the joint, and pointed at a big Spanish-style house opposite. They'd never been in a Spanish-style house. It was out of place in this neighbourhood. 'Let's . . . just . . . I wanna just . . .' He got up and started creeping towards the house. Keith followed, like he always did.

Tommy trampled a flower bed as he stomped through the yard of the Spanish house. Keith rubbed out their shoeprints in the mud with his hands.

Locked, a locked back door, but Keith checked the mat, then a flowerpot, and found the spare key, which he used to let them in. Tommy entered the house first, sniggering quietly. They came into a kitchen, then crept into the living room.

'We should really get back to Rain,' Keith said.

'Don't you want me to yourself?' Tommy replied. 'Relax,' he said.

Tommy walked over to a graduation picture of a red-headed boy with big ears, and turned it upside down, which made Keith laugh. They set about turning all the pictures in the living room upside down, even the ones that weren't hanging on the walls. Keith felt like he'd flipped a hundred pictures over, like he'd been staring at different red-headed, large-eared family members for hours. Tommy materialised behind him and picked up the photo he was about to turn.

'Dude,' said Tommy. He sat down on the sofa, transfixed by the picture. 'You have to come look at this.'

'What?' Keith sat down beside him and leant in, analysing the photo carefully. It was an old man with faded red hair, a middle-aged red-headed woman and the boy from the graduation photo – all with matching big ears, holding up a large fish. The acid gave the image a demonic cast; cultists holding their sacrifice aloft. 'I don't get it.'

'Made you look,' said Tommy. Keith looked up, and realised their faces were only inches apart, and when Tommy closed his eyes and leant in, that he'd been tricked. He didn't pull away. His mouth prickled; this was unlike a sober kiss, or even a drunk kiss. Tommy tasted like a lit joint, fresh, burning his mouth.

Keith pulled back for a breath and expected smoke to curl from his nose. Tommy's hand wound into the back of his hair; he was breathing heavily, they both were, galactic swirls of smoke on the back of Keith's eyelids when he closed them.

He could be imagining the whole thing. The joint could've hit him really hard, and he could be passed out on the sidewalk, with Tommy trying to shake him awake.

Keith opened his eyes again. He was not on the sidewalk – they were kissing. Tommy pushed him down onto the couch and straddled him.

'Yeehaw,' Keith whispered – probably shouldn't have said that aloud. Probably should've just thought it.

Tommy sitting back, and dramatically pushing a hand through his hair. Freckles melting in with the static of the night; he was glittering. He was touching Keith's dick through his jeans – smirking like Keith's boner was a *Gotcha*, like Tommy hadn't started it.

'I fucking knew it,' Tommy whispered. '*Disco cocksucker*,' he said. He came down to Keith again and bit his bottom lip. Keith hissed, at the pain and the feeling of Tommy's hands running up and down his torso.

A light flicked on above them and illuminated the stairway.

'Oh shit,' Keith said. They scrambled from the couch, Tommy falling on the floor with a thud and prompting a call of '*I have a gun!*' from upstairs. They ran out of the back door, leaving it open behind them, and vaulted the fence, both running in opposite directions as a gunshot cracked through the still, suburban night.

Keith, now alone, tore through Playa Dorada, back towards the beach, still buzzing with adrenalin, feeling oddly sober even though the lights of the still-open dive bars glittered and swirled, and the concrete at his feet sloshed around him like the tide. He stopped and caught his breath, grinning, and not-sober-enough to panic yet. Then panicking. Rain. Where was Rain?

He brought his fingertips to his lips. Tommy. He kissed Tommy.

Tommy's car. He could see it – parked up on the sidewalk by the beach. Keith staggered over to it. Maybe Tommy would be in there.

He wasn't. Keith found Rain, though, curled up on the back seat staring up at the ceiling. She looked peaceful – she looked like a little girl. Keith banged on the glass, harder than he'd meant to. He was grinning wildly, relieved. She sat up.

'Where's Tommy?' she asked. 'We were . . . kissing and then . . . He went to find you? I was too scared to leave the car.'

'I dunno where he is, we got separated.' He had a thought. 'Can you sing? Or play bass guitar?'

'What?' she said. She was starting to panic now – no need. Tommy, red-faced and out of breath, hurtled towards the car, swearing he'd been clipped by a bullet. 'You left me,' she said.

'No,' said Tommy. He looked at Keith. 'No,' he said, again. They looked at each other for a long moment.

It was Saturday now – a day off from work. If he was hungover, he'd grab breakfast with Tommy. If he wasn't, he'd pick up a new comic book or a pulpy horror novel. He'd head down to the avocado fields behind the trailer park near his and Mom's building. He'd sit by himself in a tattered armchair which had been dumped in the field a year ago and left to rot. He'd smoke, read his comics, then head back to the apartment and nap, or listen to records.

He liked his life. He was happy with his friends and his mom, and thirty hours a week stacking shelves, bagging groceries and mopping. A little bored, sometimes, a little *lacking* in something – but he figured once the band was up and running, that empty feeling would go away.

But Tommy was looking at him funny. Tommy was looking at him like he was afraid. Then Keith was afraid, too. What if they never got the band together?

'I'm gunna go home,' Keith said. Tommy worried a piece of dry skin on his lip with his teeth. 'I'm cool. Are you cool?' he asked. Tommy nodded.

★

Keith woke Mom rooting around in the fridge for something to eat. She came out of her room in a bathrobe.

'Baby boy,' she said. 'Do you want me to make you something?'

'No,' he said. He was holding an egg and a cheese single, like he was going to do something with that. 'I really don't want to go back to school.'

'Okay.'

'I want to do Si-son and Mom-funkel,' he said.

'Okay,' Mom said. 'It was Gar-mom-kel, I think. But I like yours more.' She smiled at him. 'Do you want me to do something with that egg?' He put the egg down on the counter and dropped the cheese slice. He hugged her. 'Are you high?' she asked. 'Do you feel okay?'

'I think so,' Keith said.

Shake Well

My mam won't let me squeeze my spots in the house. It's like the opposite of drinking, where she'd rather I just did it in front of her. Mam checks the mirror for pus and checks my face for scabs. She says when I squeeze my spots, I'm making my acne worse by spreading bacteria, and touching an open wound with my dirty hands – even though I wash my hands all the time. The thing is though, it's much easier to conceal a scab than it is to conceal a big, juicy lump on your face. I would maybe think about not squeezing if my spots didn't get so lumpy. But they do. So I squeeze them at school instead.

I am aware that squeezing your spots (especially in school toilets) is quite disgusting, but I think walking around with big pus-filled mountains on your chin is even more disgusting. I try to do it in the middle of lessons, so it's not busy like at lunchtime or in the morning. I ask if I can go to the toilet, and I squeeze the spots that have grown overnight. Normally they're so big, and there's so much pressure, that they splatter onto the mirror with this little shooting noise. I clean the mirror, sometimes, depending on how quick the squeezing was. Sometimes they take a really long time to come, and my face goes bright red, and even bruises a little bit where I've been squeezing. I squeeze until I run out of white stuff, and it starts to bleed.

Mam says I'll scar, and she shows me pictures of people with pit scarring and says my skin will look like that if I'm not careful. I'd still rather fill in pits than walk around with horrible white volcano spots on my face. Mam says I'll end up like my friend Cara if I'm not careful. Cara has acne, too. The pill didn't do anything, so she just went on Roaccutane *and* if that doesn't work she has to start getting it lasered. My mam says my acne isn't bad enough for Roaccutane. She doesn't like the idea of me being on the pill, either. So I'm stuck with snidey antibiotics that don't do anything, while Cara gets to nuke her face.

Mam says I just need to stop squeezing. It's a disgusting habit. But everyone has bad habits. They're normal. My boyfriend sucks his thumb. Kyle sucks his thumb so much he has a little dent in the roof of his mouth where his thumb fits perfectly. Mam says thumb-sucking is also disgusting, and worse than squeezing your spots when you're Kyle's age.

My mam thinks Kyle is only seventeen – so I reckon she'd find the thumb-sucking stuff even worse if she knew how old he actually was. I think she'd be fuming to be honest. I've been really good at making sure I say college instead of uni and to make it sound like he still lives with his mam. They'd get *so* weird if they found out about the dealing as well, even though weed is not that bad and Kyle says it's on its way to being legal.

I mean, he sells pills and powders as well but only a little bit. Normally just pills. He doesn't tell me what kind. I asked him if he sells cowies but he told me that it's lots of different pills, and no one says cowies any more. Normally he does tell people he's selling 'dancers' (which I actually think is much stupider than cowies, and just means that he *is* selling cowies) when I'm with him. They normally have nice designs on them, and my favourites are the yellow ones with a lion's face on them. A customer once complained to him that they don't do anything and Kyle and him almost had a fight in the smoking area of Propaganda at the O2. Kyle knows the bouncer so it was fine in the end. But I was scared for a bit.

After the guy said the lion-faced pills didn't work, Kyle got me to take one to see what would happen. It definitely didn't do anything but Kyle sold them all anyway. He let me keep one because I loved the lion's face and he loves me. I thought that was really lush of him, because he was charging like £20 a pill, and he only made me buy him a pint to cover it.

Kyle buys all of his stuff on the internet, because he can mark it up loads. His best customers are students, so mostly we just go around studenty areas like Heaton and Jesmond and that in his car. I like it when he lets me come with him. Sometimes we park up and do stuff, and his phone will be going crackers in the front seat, but we just ignore it.

The drugs from the internet are really cheap, and they come marked as herbal supplements and protein powder in the post. So, Kyle will pay £5 per pill, for twenty pills, and then he'll sell the pills for £20 each (or £15 or £10 if the person says he's taking the piss) so he normally makes a profit upwards of £200. I tell him all the time – he should do business studies instead of media studies.

*

I tell my mam I'm going to Cara's in West Denton tonight, but I'm actually going to Kyle's in Heaton. I've avoided getting caught by making sure I ALWAYS answer Mam's texts as soon as possible. He said he's got some orders to make and then we'll get a pizza. Pizza upsets my stomach, but I eat it anyway.

He'll drive me to school tomorrow, which I love, because no one else has a boyfriend who can drive. But he says I can't brag too much in case the school try to break us up. Like, I get the 'laws' existing and stuff, but people should really look at things like this on a case-by-case basis. I'm very mature for my age.

In the car with my mam, she looks at me and sighs. She tells me my skin looks terrible. Like that's meant to be news.

And I say to her, I tell her, I know, Mam. And she sort of does this weird laugh to herself, and she says that if I keep squeezing my spots, I'm going to end up with so many that I'll just be able to put my hands on my cheeks and *squeeze*, and my whole face will pop.

I don't say anything. She tells me not to pout. Apparently, I take myself too seriously.

Mam drops me off by the big Morrisons, and I wait till her car is out of eyeshot. Then I wait for the number 40 bus and go into town. Then, from town, I get the number 1 and go into Heaton. It takes an hour all together. I'm not sure where to get off, so I get off near the Family Shopper because I've been in it before and I know Kyle is somewhere nearby.

I get lost for a while. I have my mam's old iPhone 5c and the GPS never works. I recognise one of Kyle's customer's houses. It has a big mural on the side of random people dancing and wearing colourful clothes, and it has a broken washing machine in the yard. I knock on his door – Kyle smoked a joint with him in his kitchen, and I remember him being nice. I tell him I'm lost, and I want to go to Kyle's house. I know that Kyle lives on Cardigan Terrace, but I don't know how to get there.

The boy is really nice and walks me round to Cardigan Terrace. He tells me I was on Hotspur Street and that I probably went the wrong way when I got off the bus.

The boy asks me how old I am, and I tell him I'm seventeen. He makes a face, and asks how old I really am. So I tell him the truth. I'm fifteen. But then I tell him I'm Kyle's sister. Then he makes a face and says that's even worse because he's seen Kyle getting off with me, so I tell him I'm not actually Kyle's sister. The boy makes a funny face and tells me to be careful when he drops me off at the end of the street.

Kyle complains that I'm late – I complain that he could have picked me up. He tells me not to be a bitch. He asks me if I'm on my period.

I go straight to the bathroom and get this spot that's bubbled up on my left cheek. Right on my cheekbone. White. Makes a sound when it hits the mirror, then bleeds really heavily, but it keeps spitting pus, loads of blood and loads of pus, so I have a big streak of blood down my face. I press a tissue to it really hard, till it's stopped just enough I can fill the pit in with concealer. I pack it with powder, and give the rest of my face a brush. My skin is really bad at the moment. I try not to let it bother me, but it's so red and lumpy and ugly.

His housemate – Dean, I think – is in the kitchen with no shirt on when I come out of the bathroom, drinking tea from a chipped Sports Direct mug. He and Kyle are laughing. He asks me how my A levels are going, and then jokingly calls Kyle a paedo even though Dean thinks I'm seventeen. Kyle laughs, but not the way he laughs with me.

I tell Kyle I'm hungry, but he wants to sort his orders first. He gets me to count his cash while he connects to the dark web. I always thought the dark web was made up by adults, but it's actually real. All the URLs end in dot onion. I ask Kyle if you can really buy people on the dark web and he tells me I need to concentrate on counting. His thumb is in his mouth.

I finish counting his cash, then I come up behind him and nuzzle my nose in his hair, which I don't think he's washed recently, because it's quite greasy and it smells of sweat. I don't mind. That's how you know you're really *really* in love. I don't mind his morning breath, either.

I want to know if Kyle can buy people on the drug website. He can't. He tells me to come look. It says it's a health site. There's a section called 'Mind', which is all drugs, and a section called 'Body', which Kyle clicks on. There's steroids, skin bleach, diet pills.

And an acne treatment.

Which is $40. I google it – that's only £28. I just counted over a grand.

I want it. Kyle, I want it. Please. Please, please, *please*?

He says my skin isn't even that bad, and it won't work, and he thought I liked picking and squeezing my spots. I'm always asking to do the pimples on Kyle's back. I tell him I want to be pretty for him. He tells me I'm basically fine. I tell him I'll do more stuff to him if he gets it for me. He says I already do plenty of stuff to him. I'll go to the gym. If he buys this, I'll join a gym, and I'll go to it, since he's been pinching at my thighs and stuff and complaining I'm getting cellulite. I'll make sure I'm always totally shaved for a month.

I promise.

He puts it in the cart.

We get pizza. It makes my stomach hurt.

★

I normally put make-up on straight away in the morning, but I decide not to. Mostly because Kyle said my skin isn't that bad yesterday. When I get up and brush my teeth, I think . . . maybe it doesn't look *that* bad. I only have ten active spots, the rest is just pits and scabs and discoloration. And it's been worse before. It's not as bad as Cara's, you know?

I get back into bed. And Kyle is sitting up and looking at his phone. He tells me we have some drop-offs to do in the afternoon but once we're done, we can go into town and get Starbucks.

He says, 'Are you not going to put make-up on?' I nod. He says buying the acne stuff was probably a good idea.

★

It arrives two weeks later. The print on the label is tiny.

```
CAUTION: USE WITH CAUTION. EXTREME CAUTION IS
ADVISED WHILE USING THIS PRODUCT.
Apply to affected area with gloves. Do not spill
on fabrics. Do not use product in sunlight.
Avoid sunlight at all costs while product
processes.
Allow twenty-four hours for product to work.
Reapply treatment as needed. It is recommended
the user applies this product in private. It
is recommended the user is alone while product
processes. Should the user have concerns about
results, please consult a dermatologist.
Processing process can be distressing - caution
while using mirrors is advised.
```

Caution generally advised.
Shake well before use.

I want to use it straight away, but I decide to wait till the weekend.

I tell Mam I have food poisoning. Because I've hung on till the Friday night, she won't think I'm faking. If I did it on Sunday or Monday, she'd just think I was bullshitting to get out of school. I even make myself vomit for believability.

I wait till my parents go for their weekly trip to the Metrocentre. I shut myself up in my room, and I close the curtains. I've got supplies in my room: snacks, water, and I borrowed (stole) some Xanax from Kyle. If the treatment is *really* painful I can just knock myself out.

I squeeze a few spots for old times' sake. I think I'll miss them, but with all the shaving I'm making sure I'm doing at the moment, I have all these ingrown hairs which are even better than spots. If you leave the ingrown hairs a little while, they get just as big and nasty as normal spots, *and* you get to dig the hair out as well. Sometimes when you pull the hair out with tweezers, it has this big pus-covered root.

I put on rubber gloves, and open the bottle. It smells like hair bleach. I bleach Kyle's hair for him, and the smell always makes my eyes water. You can feel the smell right at the back of your throat, kind of caustic in your nostrils – it stings my lungs.

I squeeze it onto the glove. I think it's purple – it's hard to tell without the light. When I put it on my face, my eyes start streaming, which makes it hard to concentrate. It stings like . . . hair bleach, actually. I think acne creams do have peroxide in them – maybe it's a super concentrate, or something. Either way, it feels fizzy. On my face, it feels fizzy, and bubbly, and very itchy. But I don't scratch. Even when it starts to burn, I don't scratch. I'm not sure how much time passes.

I try to watch Netflix, but it's hard to focus. I poke my cheek, and I swear my skin gives way to my finger. I poke harder, and it's like poking the top of a cake, poking icing.

I take off the gloves. I poke where I'd poked, and my finger feels wet. I feel like I'm touching raw meat and I pull my hands away. I sit on them. I watch more Netflix, but I don't really.

My skin feels tight and too slack, all at once. Two episodes of *Riverdale* go by, and my face is stinging so much, like the worst sunburn *ever*. I touch my face again, and I swear a clump of something just comes off. It lands on the carpet with a splat. I pick it up – it's like jelly, unset jelly, those packed-lunch pots of jelly when they've been in your locker all day and they've melted. It even jiggles like jelly.

I run my fingers over my face, and all of this gloop comes off, a mask of it, and my skin has that raw, meaty feeling underneath.

I think about looking in the mirror, but I don't.

This is when I take the Xanax.

★

I wake up at around 3 p.m. the next day. I have a text from my mam.

Came in youre room this morning – decided to let you sleep. Me and dad are at big tesco hope your feeling better soon xxx

My face is stuck to my pillow.

I sit up, and the pillow comes with me. I have to peel it off, slowly, really slowly, and it hurts like picking off a scab. The pillow is covered in crusts the shape of my face. Yellow, sandy, crystally crust, the way your pimples get when they scab over while they're still weeping clear pus.

I don't open my curtains, but I pull the towel off the mirror.

The left half of my face looks like a piece of fried chicken.

But the other side, the right side is perfect. Beautiful, even. Poreless, just white, and plain, and smooth. No redness, no little purple scars, no pits, either. It's so perfect, it looks like it's been filtered.

I pick at the crust on the left side. There's more of the same beneath. More perfect skin.

Normally, I'd eat a scab like that. They're kind of inviting; they look like scraps of batter. But I decide not to in case it's poison. I scoop them up in my hands, and flush them down the toilet. I put my bedding in the washer.

I keep walking past mirrors in the house, while I'm doing bits and bobs. I'm going slowly because I'm a bit groggy from the Xanax, but I'm also going slowly because I keep stopping and looking in the mirror.

I'm actually pretty. I'm so pretty. Without all the nasty, ugly lumps, without all the red and purple marks, and pits – it's like, you're not distracted from my face any more. And you can just concentrate on my actual nose, and eyes and lips. I'm not like, Bella Hadid pretty. But I still look really good I think.

My mam is gobsmacked when she sees me. She gets back from the big Tesco, and she drops the shopping out of shock. I don't really think my dad notices, because Newcastle are playing today, but he does sort of grunt when Mam is like Look at Poppy's skin!

She says it must be the new face wash she bought me – the tea-tree-oil one. And I just agree with her, because it makes my life easier. She asks if I'm excited for Kyle to see, and I squeal because I am! I really am, and then I hear Dad shout, 'I don't like him, Poppy,' (because he really *really* doesn't) even though it's completely irrelevant to the conversation.

Mam takes a hold of my hands.

'Now, if we can get you to stop biting those nails, you'll be perfect,' she says.

★

In school, on Monday, people are also very, very surprised. First, my teacher tells me to take my make-up off, and I have to wipe my face with a tissue to prove I'm not wearing any. Then Cara spends all of first lesson demanding a list of skincare products, and she writes down everything I say, even though I'm just making stuff up.

At lunchtime, she says that maybe I was right to squeeze my spots after all, and she spends the whole hour in the toilets, squeezing her face, even though it's all sore and flakey. She doesn't even eat. I sit on the sink and eat my sandwich and watch her. I tell her she has so many spots, she could just put her hands either side of her face and squish, and maybe she'd get all of them at once. She says that's really mean.

While she squeezes, I look at my pretty new skin in the mirror. I'm so excited for Kyle to see. I texted him saying the treatment stuff worked amazingly well, and he seemed like he didn't believe me. I can't wait to rub my face in his face. He said if the acne stuff really was a dud, then I'd have to 'earn' the money he spent back. I'm sure he's joking, but I did once drop a bag of weed out the car window on the motorway (long story) and he made me wash his dishes and tidy his room for around a month.

While I'm staring at myself in the mirror, I notice a little line across my hairline. It's very thin, but it's red, and it makes a border around all of my face – like I'm wearing a mask. And when I look closely, there's a difference in the colour either side of the red line. My face is whiter, smoother, colder; my neck, my jaw and ears are all pinker – they look *fleshier* than my face does.

The bell rings. Cara is bleeding in seven different

spots – she's just letting it run all over her face. I tell her she needs to mop it up, or she'll end up with spots where the blood and the pus run. I also give her my concealer and my powder pot, and I teach her how to pack the pits with concealer and powder.

I suppose I won't need them any more, so I let her keep them.

Kyle is picking me up after school. Mam thinks I'm going to Cara's again. Kyle makes me walk down to the newsagent's at the end of the street when he's coming to get me. I trip and fall down so hard I scrape up my knees and get gravel in my palms.

Kyle isn't very far away at all – he's parked up a few metres away. He asks me if I'm okay, and I ask him why he didn't do anything, or help. He shrugs. His car smells of weed, and there's half a joint sitting on top of the dashboard. It's been stubbed out. I think he's probably just stoned and couldn't be arsed to move.

I say whatever. And he starts up the engine. He hasn't even looked at my face, or mentioned my skin or anything. I just sit for the whole journey picking gravel out of my hands, which stops me from crying, because I have something to concentrate on.

When we get to Kyle's, he tells me to stop being such a bitch. Which is unfair, because I haven't even been a bitch, I've just been sad, and I've been sad because he's been not very nice to me. I can't be arsed to argue with him. Even though weed is supposed to make you chill out, it just makes

Kyle whiny and sensitive, and generally a bit aggro, and I can't be bothered with him when he's like this. I go up to his room, and lie on his bed, and I watch YouTube on my phone. I watch beauty tutorials and think about all the nice make-up I'll do now my skin isn't horrendously red and lumpy.

Kyle comes up to his room as well, and I hope he's brought me a cup of tea or a biscuit, or one of the other things he used to give me when I was sad, but he just sits down and starts looking through the Steam sale. Kyle used to be the only person who was nice to me – and now he's barely nice to me, ever. Maybe he felt like he had to be nicer to me when we hadn't been together for as long. Now he doesn't have to impress me, and he knows I love the real him, so he doesn't have to be on guard all the time.

Still, I do miss the tea and stuff. He'd buy me things all the time as well, like teddies and hair stuff and cute bracelets and earrings. Mam and Dad found out about him because of all the presents he bought me. I had so much new stuff they thought I was stealing. They didn't stop having a go at me about shoplifting until my mam found my Facebook messages and flipped out about me having a boyfriend. I told them he was sixteen and I met him at school.

My dad wanted to break us up – even said he'd go to the police or Kyle's parents. But my mam said that would just 'martyr the relationship' and push us closer together. So they let it be.

We got together properly around my fourteenth birthday – before my skin got really bad. I ask him if he remembered how good my skin used to be, and he says not really. I get him to turn around.

Straight away he says I'm wearing make-up; I rub my face on my jumper to prove I'm not. He says he's glad it was worth the money, but he complains that I look older without the acne. He says my face looks really thin without it and complains that I look older – like that's not a good thing.

Later, when we're doing it, he makes me face away from him. I'm very, very close to the headboard. Every time he, you know, *thrusts*, I feel like I get a little bit closer to the headboard, until finally he does a couple of really *really* hard pushes, and I hit my head quite hard. I tell him to stop it because my head is hurting. He clicks his tongue at me and pulls out.

I get straight up and go to the bathroom, my forehead hurts so much. I've really banged it. I look in the mirror, expecting to see a bruise or something. I wish it was just a bruise.

There's a crack. From that thin red mark at my hairline, there's a crack running down my forehead, to my eyebrow (and my forehead is quite big, so it's a long crack) where the crack curves back up, and joins at my hairline again. It looks like a very small slice of pizza.

I try getting my nails underneath it, to see if there's any give. And there is. There's a lot of give. Once I get my nails under properly, it pops straight out, and lands in the sink, and shatters, like a plate.

I'm left with a triangle of gristle on my head – exposed, and veiny and red. I dig a couple of dusty old plasters out of their bathroom cabinet and slap them straight over the crack on my head.

I go back to Kyle's room because I don't know what else to do. I tell him he should drive me home because I hurt my head and I feel sick. He says no and get a taxi. I say I can't afford a taxi. He says he's not effing paying for it for me, and I should have thought of that before I came over. I start to cry, so he goes into his drawer and throws a tenner by my feet on the floor. I pick it up and I put my clothes on, and I go downstairs.

I have a long hard think about my relationship with Kyle, as I am not ugly any more, and could probably get a nicer boyfriend.

His housemates are in the living room smoking weed when I go down and call a taxi.

They ask me why I'm leaving, and I tell them it's because Kyle bumped my head and I feel sick. I tell them that he bumped my head while we were doing it, and that he made my head bleed and everything. I say to them that I'm really fifteen. That I only turned fifteen in April (it's May). And then Dean is like: What the fuck. And I'm like, Yeah I know, right. And Dean is like: But we've given you vodka and drugs and stuff, and I tell them to take it up with Kyle.

★

When I get home, I sneak back into the house because my mam and dad have definitely gone to bed. I'm just really quiet when I open the door, and I go up the stairs very, very slowly.

Once I'm in my room, I take off the plasters, and look at where that bit of my face fell off. I can see veins and stuff, it's very creepy. I feel really shaky. I feel like I should have more feelings about it – but it's like I'm too freaked out to freak out, you know?

I don't know what else to do, so I just tip the acne stuff straight on top of the missing bit of my face. If it fixed my acne, maybe it can fix this.

It really, really hurts. I put the plasters back over the wound to keep the liquid in place, and then I take two of the Xanax pills I took from Kyle's because I don't want to be awake for another minute.

★

I don't wake up till five the next evening. My school is actually really rubbish at keeping track of absences, especially when you ring in loads anyway, so no one rang my parents when I didn't turn up. Which is probably actually quite worrying when you think about it. Like, what if I'd been abducted, or something?

My mam and dad got in just as I was waking up, and they didn't really seem to question that I'd gotten in from school and immediately taken a nap.

When I check the mirror, that piece of my face that fell off is back. It's hard, and solid, and cold, just like the rest of my skin.

Maybe it'll be fine as long as I don't bang it. Maybe it falls off after a few weeks or something.

I wonder if I'll be stuck filling it in forever. I'm trying not to think too far ahead. I suppose I'll have to learn how to get onto the dark web. I start to worry. Have I made a mistake? Have I gotten myself in deep shit with this stupid quick fix?

I get a text from Cara, asking where I was at school today. She looks so red and pimply in her contact photo.

I decide it's worth it.

The King

Part 1: Father Forgive Me I Am a Worm

My father told me that we were once the rulers of this miserable planet. The consumption of human flesh imbued us with our victims' strength; we are young and beautiful and we live forever. We killed, we carved, we consumed and we conquered. He thought that when the current world came to its end, our people would exit our hiding and resume our natural position at the top of the food chain. Unless I'm the last one of us (which I might be). In which case . . . It's all for me, baby.

When the world ends, it'll be my time to shine. I wait in this apocalyptic whimper; I wait for another city to flood, for another tsunami, another hurricane. I wait for the bang. The nuclear bomb, the asteroid strike, some grand religious cataclysm. It was my father's wish that I be the one to restore us to our natural place – to pull down the thin curtain of human society and dominate as the light, the sun, the power.

But for the moment, I work in tech.

Officially, I am paid an insane wage to delegate work to other people, and come up with innovative, new (stupid, abstract) ways to advertise phones. Unofficially, I am just killing time until the total collapse of society.

I have sailed easily up to a senior position in marketing. As prey animals sensing something truly dangerous has entered their space, my colleagues bend to me. Their fear enables me to do silly things all day. I once spun around in my office chair till I did a big red sick on the carpet – sometimes I play hentai games on my computer, just to see if anyone will ask me to stop.

Today, we have a marketing strategy meeting for the new phone. Without me, these people are lost. They would advertise the new phone simply by describing the features of the phone, showing nice images of the phone and people using the phone. Amateur hour.

'What if we had an advert where people drop the phones into water, but the phone is fine,' I say. 'There's a girl who is both diverse and sexy in a non-threatening way. She drops the phone into a pool – and then she gets in the pool, and the phone is fine. And she takes pictures with it under the water.'

Everyone in the room nods approvingly. There is a general hum of appreciation. They are impressed.

'Innovative,' says the head of marketing. 'As always. You write the script, I'll allocate the budget.' Some Guy from Sales puts up his hand.

'My only concern here – and it's a brilliant idea by the

way – but my only concern is that while the phone is waterproof – it's not *that* waterproof,' he says.

'Right,' I say. 'But the water would be lighty-uppy. And coloured.' I pause. Everyone nods and pretends to understand how this would resolve the issue. 'So it wouldn't be like real water. It'd obviously be a metaphor,' I add.

'For what?' says a new face in the room. She is standing behind the head of marketing – probably his new assistant. I find her diverse and sexy in a non-threatening way. She doesn't seem to look at me with despair or terror in her heart. In fact, she looks at me like I am an idiot. And obviously *I* know I'm an idiot – but *she* isn't supposed to know I'm an idiot.

'For being fun and creative with your phone,' I say. The other attendees at the meeting are now confident in agreeing with me. They all nod. Someone from the creative team points and laughs at the assistant. She looks confused and upset, as if she has wandered into a madhouse.

'I'm *so* sorry about her,' says the head of marketing. 'Should I fire her?'

'No,' I say. 'Don't worry about it.' I check my watch. 'Well, I'm going to head out for my lunch break. See you.'

'We're only halfway through the agenda,' says the assistant. The head of marketing shushes her.

I have my standard lunch: two cans of diet cola. I'm a carnivore by design, not by choice. I cannot digest plant matter. I cannot even cope with animal meat. Aside from water and human flesh, diet cola is the only sustenance

I can tolerate. At home, I eat unseasoned human meat in different preparations – herbs and spices make the food intolerable to me. I can manage a little salt, but that's about it. I will eat when I get home. I will take some flesh from my current food source (who is named Roy) and I will probably eat the meat raw – either minced or in thin, fancy slices.

I don't need a lot to live. Human flesh is so nutritious for me, I can get by on a small amount – but it's been a long time since I was comfortable. The height of World War II, I think. Shortly after my father died – that's when I last felt full. My father always told me that hundreds of years ago we could eat and eat and eat. Things are too difficult now, with police forces and post-industrial societies. When people go missing, dead or alive, their relatives generally expect them to turn back up.

Things will be better when it's all over. For now, my stomach rumbles.

'Does anyone care if I go early?' I ask.

'No, ma'am,' says a man who I think is two or three paygrades above me.

I live in a penthouse apartment, which was gifted to me by a millionaire I fucked and ate – as per his request. The service charge is mental. I go to say hello to Roy, who lives on a hospital bed in the kitchen. I have him catheterised, and he came pre-fitted with a stoma bag – which I personally find easier to clean than a bedpan. He lies in bed all day, reading the books and magazines I leave for him, and he also has an iPad. I have all the subscriptions, so he can watch pretty much anything he wants. This all seemed like a fair exchange for his legs. I am currently making my way up his left arm.

'Hello, Roy,' I say.

'Kill me,' Roy says.

'Not today, Roy!' I reply. 'How long till the end?'

'Sixty-three days. *Please* kill me before it comes.'

Roy is an interesting case, in that he's both a purveyor of doomsday prophecies, and a sick, disgusting pervert who wants to be slowly eaten alive. I first found him on a doomsday prophecy subreddit, where he was posting his doomsday prophecies. He made lots of correct predictions. He's predicted all sorts of natural disasters, and all major points of escalation in hostilities with Russia. Ultimately, he thinks we'll go nuclear before the world boils. And then he thinks we'll be plunged into a permanent nuclear winter. This is fine with me; I prefer the cold to the heat.

I, like many on the subreddit, had taken note of the accuracy of his prophecies. I had no intention to contact him, until I saw the same username on a dark web cannibal fetish website. I was like . . . No way is this DoomSayerRoy from Reddit. So I messaged him. I said: *OMG are you the DoomSayerRoy? From Reddit?*

And he said: *All I want to do is have a beautiful horrible woman eat me before the end of the world I am begging you to eat me none of these people are serious but I can tell you are please please tell me you're serious?*

And I told him I was serious. Not only was I serious –
I was this planet's Apex Predator. When he met me, he said:
*You will become like a god after the end. You will lead my
species to its oblivion.* And I said: *Ha ha, cool.*

I climb into Roy's hospital bed and stroke his bald head.

'Tell me about the end, Roy,' I say.

'When the firestorms end, a black snow will come. Then
grey, then white again. A virgin's bridal veil, thrown over
the raped and ravaged body of the earth. You will stain it
red.'

'Neat,' I say. 'I love you, Roy.'

'Your kind cannot truly love one so lowly as me.'

This was true – but I could love him the way a farmer
might love a really big cow or something.

★

The assistant who seems invulnerable to the devastating
power of my presence is named Shauna. Her lack of reaction to me is fascinating, but she avoids me like the plague.
Not like she's frightened of me – but like she can't be
bothered with me. I don't speak to her again until the
thirty-second day before the end. Lots of people in the office
are gathered around the television, watching a particularly
troubling news report about the USA. Roy told me this
would happen a few weeks ago. I am playing *Dramatical
Murder* (an erotic visual novel) at my desk and don't pay
attention to the TV.

Shauna is behind me.

'Is that porn?' she says.

'As far as I'm concerned, this is among humanity's greatest artistic achievements,' I say. I turn around, and look at her, looking at me. Where's the panic? Where's the sweat? I move suddenly and she doesn't flinch! 'What gives, what's up with you?'

'What do you mean?'

'Like, why aren't you scared of me?' I ask. 'You a fellow member of the master race?' This makes Shauna blink really hard and wind her chin back into her neck in shock. Shauna isn't white and I am (well, I'm fair-skinned, I should say! As a non-human entity, human racial categories do not apply perfectly to me) so I probably should've chosen my words a bit more carefully.

'So you're a pervert and a fucking Nazi?' she asks.

That's totally inaccurate. I was all over the place during World War II. Didn't do any fighting. Though I am immune to fire and bullets and have an inherent lust for violence, I didn't have the time for battlefields. There were settlements where the streets were running red with human blood – where bodies were scattered about the place like Easter eggs.

'Oh, no. I was asking if you were one of Us. You know . . . The Few. The Apex Predators,' I say. She looks confused. 'Are you a super-strong, immortal primate who subsists on human flesh?'

'Excuse me?' she says. She stares at me, and at the anime dicks on my monitor.

'You've got no idea what I'm talking about,' I reply. I toss my computer mouse at her suddenly – she catches it. Super-fast reflexes. 'Can you eat human food without throwing it back up? Maybe you're like . . . a hybrid. A daywalker! Do you have a mysteriously absent parent? Oh, or were you raised by someone very secretive who never seems to age?'

'Goodbye,' says Shauna. Christ, Shauna is absolutely *no* fun. If she's not a daywalker, I don't know what's going on with her. I hope she doesn't survive the apocalypse – because she seems like a total bore. I hear my father's disappointed voice ringing in my head. I should've challenged her to single combat. Whoever loses has to have their head cleanly removed from their body – the most inconvenient injury my people can suffer. If our lizard-like regeneration abilities can be slowed or stopped, beheading can even be fatal!

I feel ashamed. But I also feel that all this 'single combat' stuff was what led to the devastation of our species in the first place.

Later in the day Shauna reports me to management. She brings the head of marketing over to my desk, and points at the pornography on my screen and says I was talking about the master race.

'Don't be such a square, Shauna,' says the head of marketing.

Shauna quits the next day. Sad!

★

We are on the penultimate day of the world as we know it, according to DoomSayerRoy. I have spent most of the previous weeks doing bunker admin. Charging battery packs, sorting out little generators, downloading and stockpiling television shows, books, music and films on external hard drives. I download lots of games, too. I feel like I've created my own little Library of Alexandria. This is mostly for after the fall. I'm hoping to hibernate for a while – poke my head back out when the worst of the radiation has died down. I'm immune to the effects of nuclear fallout – but only to a point. Found that out the hard way after Hiroshima. Worst stomach ache I've ever had.

I have also stockpiled hundreds and hundreds of cans of diet cola – once I'm out, I expect I'll never drink it again. This will be the one truly sad loss from the old world. I also have a big freezer – this is where I'll be putting Roy, once I kill and butcher him.

'Well, Roy,' I say, pulling out the big knife Roy requested I kill him with. 'It's been a hoot.'

'Will you go to the bunker tonight?' he asks.

'No. I want to be here when the party starts,' I say. 'I'm going to go to work – watch the panic break out. Then I'll go down.'

'I'm really happy for you,' he says.

'I'm happy for you, too.'

Roy wants me to hang him upside down, cut his throat and exsanguinate him like a pig. He wants me to cut off his dick and balls before he goes.

The dick-and-balls thing – they never enjoy that as much as they think they will. It's always such a let-down for them. It's a little sad. When I do it, he really doesn't like it, and begs me to slit his throat.

Farewell, Roy, I hardly knew ye. I butcher him carefully, vacuum seal all of his bits and stick them in the freezer. I hope one day to come across another with such a clear gift of prophecy. I post about his demise to the doomsday prophecy Reddit.

Pour one out for my boy, Roy. He died doing what he loved (being eaten alive and straight up jerking it). Hope you fuckers enjoy the fireworks tomorrow. Most of you will die. Your gods will die with you. Meek will inherit the earth? Don't think so. The PEAK will inherit (that's me) – maybe see you in a few years!!!

The next day at work, I'm so excited. I drink a full two-litre bottle of diet cola and openly eat Royflesh at the office, which no one bats an eyelid at, because they're all freaking out and looking at their phones and then turning the television on. I can't believe these losers actually came to work – the entire species is cucked beyond belief. On the television the prime minister gravely announces that one of Russia or the USA has made a nuclear strike on the other.

'Oh, yippee!' I say. Everyone looks at me. 'Mutually assured destruction, baby! You know what that means!' I grab my jacket and approach the nearest member of staff. I kiss her on the mouth and tear her throat out with my teeth. The prey scatters, screaming and bustling out of the office, back to their pathetic little families, knowing that most of them will die.

As I skip out of the office, I think very vaguely of Shauna. What was her deal, anyway?

Part 2: There Can Only Be One

Want to hear something interesting about me?

I saw Elvis live in Vegas *fifty-seven* times. The first ten to twenty times, I was in awe. *There he is.* The king of rock 'n' roll is right in front of your face, shaking his dick around and playing all the hits. Even at the time it felt like something special, you know? Seeing the biggest star of a generation (even from an inferior race) up close like that – it felt big. I felt like a part of history.

But once the novelty wore off, all I could see was how tired he looked. Didn't dance like he used to, seemed kind of short of breath, jittery and exhausted. Dawned on me how many consecutive nights he'd played, how sick of playing Vegas he must have been. And I started asking around and found out his manager had trapped him in this nasty contract, wouldn't let him tour, wouldn't let him stop.

And then I realised Elvis was no more the king of rock and roll than a zoo lion was the king of the jungle. Not to belabour the metaphor, but he paced up and down that stage like a caged animal. And I didn't just pity him, I empathised with him. Here I was, one of planet Earth's most glorious creatures, living in this perverse state of restraint! Unable to murder murder murder kill kill kill the way Nature intended.

But now it's been . . . Gosh, what . . . like a hundred and fifty years since the bombs fell? And you'll be pleased to hear that I've assumed my natural place at the top of the food chain. It's Viva Las MEgas, baby!

I went down to the bunker, ate all of my Roy then went to sleep for a century. When I climbed out, I was honestly worried I'd be by myself – you know? Like I'd let it run alone for too long and all the remaining humans killed each other long before I had a chance to have my fill.

But no – I found a settlement pretty quickly. And it sucked there – it was so normal. All clean and organised and stuff. I asked them if there was anywhere more fucked I could go. Once they were done freaking out about a person suddenly turning up after a century with no idea what was what – they pointed me to somewhere real messed up and dangerous. I even intimidated them into giving me a car, so I could take all my cool electronics with me.

The settlement was called *New Hope* when I first found it. I renamed it *Dad City* in honour of my father. Dad City is in the remains of a huge, fantasy-themed theme park. It was once named King Arthur's Fun Zone – it survived the bombs because it was in the middle of nowhere. The whole park is gated and has an on-site hotel.

But despite living in a sick post-apocalyptic theme park, they'd all gone a bit 'last five minutes of *Threads*'. Literacy limited, returned to a sort of feudal system – a lot of like 'Oh woe is me I have only one limb left and bandits raped my three-armed baby.' They wore the tattered remains of employees' medieval costumes and made new clothes in the shape of the old costumes. Rancid vibes – ideal for me, though.

They were being ruled by a tyrannical king named Golden. He was keeping a (super-problematic) harem of teenaged girlwives and boywives, he executed people on a whim and made his subjects beat the shit out of each other for his amusement.

I get that humans lowkey love to be subjugated, but I honestly didn't understand why they hadn't overthrown Golden yet. There were tens of them – only one of him. No self-respecting member of a salvageable species would just bend over and take that not-so-iron fist, not when he was so spectacularly outnumbered. I lost the last of my faith in humanity in New Hope. They wanted to get cucked so badly? Then I'd be the cuckoo.

I established my dominance quickly. I entered their community as an 'envoy from the past' – I earned Golden's trust by showing him some of the pornography I had saved.

Behind his back, I whipped the peasants up into a frenzy. Within two weeks of my arrival, I was leading them to his palace (which was the penthouse suite in the on-site hotel) in the dead of night. We broke down the door and busted into his bedroom. But before the mob could descend upon him, I had them halt. A show of mercy?

Nah.

'He's not your tyrant any more,' I told them. I snapped Golden's neck with my bare hands. I smashed open his skull and ate his brains with my fingers. I turned to the peasants and said: 'I am. And I can do this to any one of you, whenever I like. And if you try to rise up against me you will fail for I am unkillable. I'll crush and eat you all. I am your new god and you will bow down before me.'

They all fell to their knees.

'Ha ha,' I said. 'Neat.'

★

For a century, I brought them stability. I brought them agriculture, I taught them how to battle the nuclear winter which had long since claimed the land. Generators, hothouses – they barely knew how to hunt. Golden had them living on salvaged crap, rats and human flesh. I taught them human flesh was a meat for kings, not peasants, and showed them how to grow corn and apples and shit.

I say *I* showed them. In my Library of Alexandria, I had saved many many hours of instructional videos on things like farming, building a basic infrastructure – survival stuff. It took a generation of peasants to get things on track – but once their children were grown enough to handle a cheeky bit of construction, it was pretty much business as usual. Humans were really at their happiest on the brink of destruction. They were so occupied with farming and keeping the heat on – basic survival stuff – that they didn't have time for fear, for existential dread, for the kind of petty squabbles that developed into deep prejudice, that curdled into war and violence and mass murder. That stuff was my job.

While they farmed, I colonised. Avoiding functional settlements where I could – I scouted the lands for savages, and whipped them into shape. In Dad City, they became functional on punishment of death. If I had any pushback, I'd kill and eat dissenters in front of everyone in the throne room. They submitted to me. They knew my glory. They expanded Dad City to fill the entire grounds of the theme park – and even began to build beyond the fence. Outer Dad City became a vast farmland – inner Dad City was the cradle of a new civilisation. Scientists and engineers learned from the knowledge of the past to build a new future. A new future built in service to me. Their God-King.

Soon I didn't need to scout. People came to Dad City for comfort, for safety, for the protection of the Divine Being who ran the place with an iron fist if needed.

And it was with one of these ragtag groups that she returned to me. Shauna – unmarred physically by time and the horrors of the end of the world but deeply mentally scarred. She looked the same – but with much worse hair and clothes. Bit dead behind the eyes as well.

She demanded to see the king of Dad City – knowing, I think, who she would meet. She came with a handful of sick children from a settlement she'd been running. To hear her people tell the story, she'd shown up fifty years ago and they'd instinctively put her in charge. But they lacked my knowledge and resources. When she heard there was a cannibal goddess running an advanced settlement to the north – she guessed she'd find me.

'I *knew* it!' I said. 'I *knew* you were one of us. One of me.' I embraced her like an old friend. She seemed haunted. Probably because she lived through the nuclear bombs and stuff. Shame – if she'd recognised her divinity back then, I probably would've let her in the bunker.

'What am I?' she asked. 'I . . . I thought I had an inflammatory bowel disease. I went weeks without food after the bombs and didn't die. I ate irradiated human flesh, and I was *fine*. It's all I've eaten since.' Didn't even say hello. Rude, but also assertive – I liked that. 'Why? Why don't I die? Why am I immune to radiation? Why does normal food make me so sick? What *is* this?'

She had a lifetime of questions. Several lifetimes' worth, in fact. I gave her all the answers I could. Cheerfully. She seemed to take it well. I asked her to apologise for calling me a white supremacist at the office two hundred years ago and she said, 'Whatever, I guess.'

I gave Shauna a tour of Dad City. Showed her the restored tech, the roller coaster we run once a year for important ceremonial reasons (I think it's fun). I showed her our hothouses, our crops, our infirmary, our nursery. I showed her the way I had stewarded them, the life I had given them, the fair and reasonable god I had become in the new world. This settlement was a wretched hive of rape, disease and violence before I came.

'And there's no rape or violence from you?' she asked, sceptically. We were in front of the shed where I keep my human cattle. You could tell because of the screams, and the sign that says *human cattle shed*. I shrugged.

'The food,' I pointed to the shed. 'That's just for me. And all of the guys in there suck. Bandits, raiders who didn't know what they were in for.'

'And that's it?' Shauna pressed. I struggled to lie to her. Perhaps her mental powers had outstripped mine.

'I keep like *two* sex slaves,' I said. 'But it's on a rotational basis and they *do* volunteer for the position.' Shauna pursed her lips at me. 'Okay, fine, I make them do like a "'Lottery' by Shirley Jackson" thing every six months' Keeps them on their toes. And it's good to know who's popular!'

'Jesus Christ,' said Shauna. She pinched the bridge of her nose, and kept walking with me. I took her back to the main-hall-slash-throne-room, where I was *slightly* embarrassed to find my sex slaves waiting by the throne, all naked and stuff. There were four of them – two men and two women (names irrelevant) – who were waiting patiently for the 3 p.m. orgy. My serving staff also waited patiently – unsure whether this would be an occasion where I'd like them to stay and watch. I dismissed everyone except the sex slaves. I sat on the throne (plastic and salvaged from the original theme park) and Shauna stared at me.

I felt very judged by her. Kink-shamed – in *my* post-apocalyptic kingdom, where kink-shaming had been banned for a century! I wasn't used to it. Still, I had a proposal for her. I told her to bring her people here. Let us pool our resources – let Shauna rule by my side, taking her rightful place as the divinely ordained king of a whole city, not some glorified mayor of a rickety crickety settlement.

She said no.

'Why not?' I asked. I felt hurt.

'Why don't I want to do slavery and orgies and murder with you?' She sounded so *indignant*, like she found me repulsive. 'You're an irony-poisoned, edge-lord piece of shit. Why not help them rebuild? Why not . . . do something positive, creative, meaningful?' she said.

'I am helping them rebuild. It was fucking awful here before. I've made some real strides for women, particularly. Full equality – in fact, we've kind of swung the other way into misandry. We say *jilling off* here instead of jacking off. Ultimately, I'm rebuilding things as they should be. With us at the top, you know?' I said.

'What happened to *us*? Not you and me, but our species?' she asked. She sounded sharp. It was like she already knew the answer. 'What happened when *we* were at the top?'

'We all killed each other,' I admitted. 'Did loads of wars. When there were fewer of us, too few to hold a kingdom down, we killed each other in little minor territory struggles. Then in single combat and stuff.' I thought for a moment. I had a counter-argument for this very valid point. 'But at least we're not an inherently cucked species! I'd rather die with dignity in single combat. They'd all rather live their parasitic little lives than fight back. And that's how I was before the fall. But not now. Now I've assumed the role I was born for. And you could assume it with me. Help me repopulate the earth with the master race!' I said. 'And please know that when I say *master race*, I mean immortal cannibals of all colours, not white people.'

Shauna did not seem positive or negative here, only exhausted. She squinted at me, like I was talking an absolute load of bollocks, and not the gospel truth.

'We're both . . . cis women,' she said.

'Oh, so you've *assumed* I'm cis?' I fired back. She blinked at me and pointed out that I was visibly pregnant. I would've been about sixth months along with my third Lil Hellraiser at that point. I was only fertile around once every two decades – children did not particularly interest me. I handed them off to wet nurses and allowed them to distinguish themselves. I'd be interested if they chose to become interesting. 'He's got plenty of jizz. So does he.' I nudged my male sex slaves with the toes of my boots. They squeaked, as I had instructed them to do when I touched them. '*Ideally* we'd get into some kind of master-race polycule with a dude of our own species but this'll do for—'

Shauna cut me off. 'Jesus fucking Christ,' she said. She began to leave the throne room. I followed her.

'Shauna, I hate to break this to you . . . but if you reject me and keep working with a rival group . . . we will have to shift to *Highlander* rules,' I said.

'What does that mean?' she asked. I laughed at her for

not having seen *Highlander*. 'I've seen *Highlander*, I just don't know what you're on about.'

'*There can only be one*,' I said. 'One kingdom, one king.'

'I think it's there can *be* only one, not there can *only be* one,' she said, like I didn't perfectly remember the film I'd built a lot of my personal philosophy around.

'I'm afraid I'm challenging you to single combat,' I said. Shauna stopped dead and looked at me with her mouth wide open.

'But you *just* said—' Then she stopped. Cut herself off, shook her head. 'No. No, I'm going, I'm not doing this.' She opened the door, and tried to leave.

'Seize her!' I called to my sex slaves. They ran at her, genitals and breasts bouncing in an amusing way.

'Fuck off,' Shauna snapped. 'Don't seize me, go away,' she said. And the sex slaves halted at her command, torn between the opposing voices of two masters they were compelled to obey. I made a threatening gesture to let the slaves know they were in deep shit, and ran after Shauna as she left the throne room.

'Oh come on, Shauna, don't be like that!' I called, following her into the cold. 'It's really offensive to our culture to refuse to engage in a battle to the death!'

'I'm not fighting you to the death while you're pregnant,' she shouted. The wind howled. It was dark – Shauna's superior face was illuminated in my floodlighting. I realised that her eyes were the colour of my beloved diet cola, and that I could not stand to let her go, nor could I stand to kill her. It was lonely at the top. And here we were – the last of our kind, refusing to embrace each other. We were blood brothers. She knew it. If we did not come together now, we would always find each other.

'What are you, sexist or pro-life or something?' I tried. Shauna rolled her eyes at me. She did not move. Did she feel it, too? I begged. For the first time in my life, I fell to my knees and begged. I took her hand in mine. 'Okay, okay, no single combat. But what if you just stuck around for like a week? Saw what it was like to live in your natural state. Like a king. Doesn't your blood call you to it? To dominate? To consume? Don't they disgust you, the way they fall in line, the way they bend for you? You can't love them; you can only pity them. They cannot love you, only fear you. But we could . . . We're equals, Shauna. We could be something,' I said. No irony-poisoning, no references to jilling off – pure sincerity. I almost wanted to throw up.

'I don't want to be like you,' Shauna said. 'You're really unpleasant.'

'Maybe you'll be a good influence on me?' I said. 'Your people will get my resources – and you can keep me in line.'

'What if you drag me down with you?' she asked.

'You might like it,' I told her.

Part 3: God Cares About These Helpless Mortals
(or: The Time Before the Porn Wars)

I was executed by Shauna some thirty years after she joined my kingdom. In many ways I was hoist by my own petard.

Now I bet you're wondering – did she punish you? For being a dick? For being super-annoying? No! As I always suspected I might, I dragged Shauna down to my level. And she was more powerful than me. Quickly, she became the tyrant she was born to be – her will to dominate flourished under my tutelage, and it was not long before she had dominated me. And that was fun for a while – I had never been beneath someone before. Not since my father had I played second banana to a more powerful Apex Predator – and under Shauna, that second-banana position came with a thrilling new sexual role. I was a bottom! Imagine being the ultimate femdom for centuries then getting out-strapped by your own mentee!

I couldn't even begrudge the coup. In the same way that I had killed and eaten my father all those centuries ago, I expected Shauna would kill and eat me. I did have numerous fail-sons and lame-daughters over the years – but all of their will combined paled in comparison to Shauna's. Her children were more powerful than mine. Her line will inherit. *There can only be one*, I guess. When she came with the humans, with our children too, to string me up, I was proud.

'Good job, Shauna!' I said. 'Slay me!' And she told me

to shut up. She put my neck on the block (a prop from the original theme park) and revved up her chainsaw. She told me she'd been waiting centuries for this. That I was a scourge and a disease, and she would lead the humans into a new age of enlightenment. No more war, no more suffering – peace at the cost of a meal here and there for Shauna. Even my ungrateful fail-kids were on board with her plan.

She sliced off my head. So long, Las MEgas, we had a good run!

The thing is – I didn't die. She thought we were running on *Highlander* rules with regard to our deaths, as well. Figured a beheading would be the end of me. But no – not with our super-fast regeneration abilities. She chopped off my head, and I regrew my body within hours. I wasn't about to tell her she had to eat me. I was proud of her, but I wasn't stupid. After a hanging, a drowning, a burning and her stabbing and poisoning me a bunch of times, she tried starving me to death, chaining me up in a barn and leaving me to the elements. But I just got angry – I busted out of the barn they were keeping me in, ate a bunch of peasants and ran off into the night.

I was tragically forced to leave my massive library of pornography (now central to the culture of Dad City) behind. I ran to the coast, took to the sea, swam the stretch of ocean to the continent and set up home there. I did not speak the language, and brute-forced the helpless freaks there into speaking mine. Again, I kept away from sane settlements – found a bunch of mutant weirdos, christened them Dad City II and told them I would be ruling them from now on.

I drew them a picture of Shauna – I told them she was their target. I told them we would struggle together, and reclaim the pornography (and other knowledge, I guess) she had stolen from me. Their wills were too weak not to fight for my moronic cause. They did not overthrow me. They trained and worked to spill their blood for me. And soon we will cross the ocean. We will dethrone Shauna, and annihilate the haters and losers of the original Dad City – we will send her off into the night and she will rise again.

All the humans in our wake will submit to their roles in our endless struggle for dominance. It's like they do not realise there are more of them than there are of us. Fifty of them against one of us? No contest. They might lose some of their numbers, but would it not be worth it? Not for them, I guess. They fear their measly lives ending at our hands and are grateful for the scraps we feed them. Food, warmth, ancient porn; living on their bellies when they could die on their feet with dignity.

Perhaps the denizens of Dad City II will put it together. Maybe I'll be on Dad City V or VI before the revolution comes. Till then, Shauna and I will have our pissing contests, and they'll drown in our piss.

Company Man

The dream starts like this:

I am wading through knee-deep snow. Everything below the knee is numb, my flesh like sponge around the bone. It is night. My skin is as blue as my dress. The snow, too, is blue and studded with crystals and glittering in the moonlight. I fall. I push on. My destination is the red tent some way ahead of me. Wind carries its music to my ears.

I had this dream for years before I made it to the tent. Every night I got a few yards closer. Even now, there will be nights where I die in the snow.

Tonight, I reach the tasselled flap of the tent. I smell straw and smoke and animal shit.

I pull it back—

And I wake up to the sound of my alarm ringing. My pillow wet with drool. My heart thudding.

There is no rest for the wicked, so I leave my bed. I brush my teeth until my gums bleed. I spit pink foam into the sink. I comb my hair. It is bobbed and black and anonymous. I put in contact lenses. I apply moisturiser and soft, professional make-up. As the day goes on, the make-up will gather in and crack around these new lines in my forehead. Worry lines. No joyful crow's feet or marionette lines; below the brow my skin is as smooth and taut as a mask.

I put on clothes that are drab and cheap. I take the bus to the job my father arranged for me. I work for the party because my father is a party man. At my job, I will organise other people's meetings, and I will order the office supplies and I will attend meetings and write minutes. And I will receive a hang-up call, as I do every day, and it will send a cold chill down my spine.

I do; it does. The office accountant looks over to me when the phone rings.

'Your ghost caller, Dora?' she asks. I nod. 'We'll have to call the phone company.'

'Yes, it's probably a problem down our end,' I reply – because there's no reason Dora should be receiving strange hang-up calls. But Martina might get them – there are plenty of reasons someone would want to harass Martina on the phone.

Shortly after the hang-up call, a man I have never seen comes into the office. I feel the same cold, paranoid fear I do when the phone rings and no one is at the other end. Though the man looks completely normal. But it is normal for a telephone to ring, isn't it? I ask if I can help him – he nods.

'I'm from the water company,' he says. 'I think I have a meeting here today.'

I check the calendars I keep for the party officials. As I scan the calendars, I look up at the man. He is older than me by at least a decade. Clean-shaven and neatly dressed, he rocks on his heels. He is of average height. I find him unobtrusively handsome and a little too thin.

'Hold on,' I say. I flip through the calendar of the most relevant official. 'Oh. It's the same day next month.' I show him the calendar. The man closes his eyes, squeezing them shut tightly, as if the news pains him. His eyes are nice. A bright hazel. The colours of a park as they are now in autumn. 'We can't fit you in today – I would if I could.'

'Don't worry,' he says. 'I'm so sorry to have bothered you. I'll be back on the correct day.'

I watch him walk away.

When I go out for lunch, I bump into him in the park. It is getting too cold and wet to eat outside, but I like to watch the ducks splashing around in the pond as I eat. The ducklings I'd watched over spring and summer are gone now, either indistinguishable from the adults or dead.

I eat a cold potato salad from a plastic tub. My fingers sting around the fork – going red and white in the bitter wind.

The man from the water company is watching the ducks, too. It seems to take a moment for him to notice me.

'Hello,' he says. I wave because my mouth is full. 'I'm delaying going back to the office. They won't be happy with me.'

'Tell them he's sick and you had to reschedule,' I say. 'It's true, you know. He's not even here today. I'm sorry I didn't say so earlier – but you left quickly.'

'Oh,' says the man. 'That's a relief. I suppose I should get back.' I wave again. He begins to walk away from me, then turns on the spot. 'My office is just over there,' he says, pointing at the water company building. 'Maybe I'll see you here again?'

'You probably will, yes,' I reply. He leaves without giving me his name.

At home, I eat soup I made the previous day. I watch the nightly broadcast – tonight, a ballet and the news. The news says that all is well. The country is stable. Our distant war proceeds with minimal casualties. The economy flourishes. The people are healthy and beautiful and prosperous. The television turns itself off when the broadcast is complete. I make a tea and I read a book and I think about the man from the water company.

My father calls me late in the evening while my mother is in bed. He speaks to me in a low voice, as if I were his mistress and not his daughter.

'How was work today, Marti?' he asks. My own name sounds foreign to my ear. I am Dora now. It is only to Papa and my probation officer that I remain Martina. My father is sort of like a second probation officer – he doesn't really want to know about my day, he just wants to hear that I'm sober and out of trouble.

'Fine, Papa,' I say. I give him a short run-through of the

day – I don't mention the man from the water company.

'Good,' he says. He doesn't tell me anything about his day and avoids answering me when I ask about my mother.

The book I have to read isn't very good, so I go to bed and have the dream again.

This is what happens when I make it to the tent:

I push through the flap – I am always expecting a circus, but instead, I enter a cabaret. A dimly lit, lushly decorated space with strings of lights and thick rolls of red fabric hanging from the ceiling. The walls and ceiling are red as well; the light takes on a warm quality. There are tables where blurry, indistinct, richly costumed spectators drink and eat and laugh. They all wear masks – feathered, long-beaked – and they all look at me as I pass them. I am looking for the stage.

The master of ceremonies, the musicians and the dancers beckon me towards it. The emcee points up to a huge cage, suspended by a chain from the ceiling. When the cage rattles I wake up.

I dress. I commute. I work. At lunch, I go to the park hoping to see the man from the water company. He is there, drinking soup from a thermal flask.

'Oh, hello,' he says. 'I didn't get your name yesterday.'

I say Dora, because that is the name on my passport and the name I use at work. I hardly ever slip up and call myself Martina. I always answer to Dora.

'Lev,' he replies.

'Did you get in trouble, yesterday?'

'No. I'm glad he really was sick. I'm a terrible liar,' he says. 'I couldn't even lie about homework at school. People are always telling me I overshare. I'm just candid by nature, I suppose.' He looks at me and blinks – I could swear he'd gone a little pink, were he not already pink with the cold. 'Sorry – excuse me.'

'It's fine,' I say. I'm charmed by him. Whether this is because Lev is charming, or because my standards are low, I am not sure. Most of the men I speak to are small-time party officials who are my father's age. And Martina was easy to impress. Martina used to bat her eyelashes at anyone who paid her any mind. Dora's a little more conservative than that – so I smile, hoping to look girlish and coy.

I want Lev to tell me that he came to the park in the hope he would see me. I will tell him then that I'd hoped to see him. I hope he will ask me out. I try not to look at him like a dog begging for scraps at the dinner table. His eyes are even brighter in the daylight. They're heavily lashed; his nose is hooked and striking, and his lips are shapely – neither full nor thin. If my dreams didn't lead me through the snow into that tent, I'm sure they would lead me to a man who looked like this.

'In the spirit of being too candid,' he says, clearing his throat and fastening the lid back on his flask. 'I was hoping to see you again. I usually eat lunch at my desk.' I say *oh*, playing innocent and dumb. If I were to say *oh* in a tone too knowing or flirtatious, I would surely put him off. 'Are you married?' he asks. I shake my head.

'I was. He passed away,' I tell him. Miss Martina Kirsch might be unmarried at thirty-one but Mrs Dora Novak (née Kirsch) was tragically widowed four years ago, and came to the capital to restart her life. How upset Dora is about the death of her fictional husband depends on the audience and my mood. To the people at the office – I am still too distressed by my loss to discuss it. Dora's husband (who I must remember is named Tomas) was a saint who died suddenly, shockingly, of an undiagnosed heart defect. The cause of death and the name are always the same – but if I speak to a man, alone, one may find Tomas becoming cold, and cruel. One may find me ambivalent, looking for company.

'Oh,' he says. 'I lost my wife as well. Years ago now, but . . .' He trails off. I give him an understanding smile. Dora knows what this is like. 'Would you like to have dinner with me?'

I smile and nod, looking down at the floor. A performance. We exchange home phone numbers – Lev says that he will call me. He will tell me the time and the place.

Tonight, the broadcast is a recording of a classic play – one that makes me cry, because it is about a pair of doomed lovers. I imagine Lev and myself in the main characters' places. The news says once again that everything is fine. My father does not call. I read an old women's magazine with lists of tips: 'How to fool him with your make-up'; 'How to impress on the first date'. I feel young, and silly. I fall asleep reading about the ways I can highlight my body's best features without looking loose.

In tonight's version of the dream, I do not want to go to the tent. I don't want to see who is onstage, or what is in the cage. I stand in the snow and freeze to death.

★

I put on too much make-up before the date, so I take it off and do it again. Heavy foundation and red lipstick do not suit me. I look old and cheap. Martina might wear this, but Dora wouldn't. He asked me out with a face that was almost bare – so I use the same base I would for work, then put on a little more mascara than I usually would and a pink lipstick, and I decide that this is good. I look nice. Dora looks nice.

I pin my hair away from my face with a pair of good, ceramic hair clips. They are pearly white and the size of my finger. I forget, sometimes, how pretty I am. How pretty Dora can be when she tries. It has been a while since Martina has been made up – and Martina didn't know how to work with her natural beauty. She always painted herself up like a cheap floozy.

I wear a blue dress – one that looks like the dress from my dream. Blue satin cut below the knee. I put on flesh-coloured tights and dark-blue shoes. I carry a dark-blue handbag and wear a dark-blue coat. I look neat and fashionable in a way that is timeless, not trendy.

Lev said to meet him at a restaurant – one serving foreign food. No one has ever taken Dora out on a date. The men who hear Dora's sob story don't want to spoil her – they're glad to get permission to fuck her and more comfortable knowing they're not spoiling some geriatric maiden or befouling another man's wife. They can convince themselves they're doing her a favour. And she's fine with that, for the most part. The kinds of things that would cause Martina to drink herself into a stupor roll over Dora like water off a duck's back. Dora likes things with no strings attached. Dora is stable and knows what she wants. Dora is an island.

He is already at the restaurant when I arrive. He leaps up to take my coat; my heart leaps up into my throat. He is wearing a nice shirt and a nice sweater and nice trousers. He tells me I look lovely. We have spoken only a few words to each other, and I am probably already in love with him. If Dora is an island – Martina is marooned and waits with desperation for another castaway.

Conversation between Lev and I flows as easily as the wine. We both order the same type of wine – and we both want to order the same appetiser (bruschetta) then decide to also get our second choice (we both wanted artichokes) and share them. Well – Dora wanted the artichokes, like Lev did. Martina wanted garlic bread, even though it's stupid to get two bread-based appetisers.

We also both order the same main meal.

'Our tastes must be similar,' I say.

We talk about our lives. Agree to get each other's sad stories about our dead spouses out of the way early, to make sure their presence does not hang over the date.

Dora says:

I met Tomas in high school, and we got married right after graduation. We had trouble having children. He blamed me even though the doctor said Tomas had problems and I didn't. He became more and more bitter and distant, then died suddenly of an undiagnosed heart condition. I have been lonely without him – but I was lonely with him, too.

Lev says:

I met Lilija in school, but we did not reconnect until after university. I was born in the capital and came back here to work for the national water company – she was working there, too, as a technician, and I was – I am – an engineer. We were married. We had a son. Our son died in a terrible accident. Lilija was diagnosed with a treatable cancer, but refused help and died several years ago, after a short, ugly illness.

'How awful,' I say. 'I'm so sorry, Lev.'

'To lose a child like that . . .' He shakes his head. 'It's catastrophic. I'm not the same man I was when I met Lilija. She was like a different person when she died, too. Bitter, twisted. I've been lonely, too,' he says. 'I know what that's like. To be with someone, and to be so lonely. It's almost better when they're gone, isn't it? You can really grieve what you already knew you'd lost.'

I nod. Or Dora nods, because Martina doesn't understand this feeling at all. Martina feels guilty and sick when she hears this, so I tune her out. Dora knows loss well and feels it, and I focus on Dora's feelings until I tear up. Lev reaches over and holds my hand. I could cry at the contact – the first time a man has touched (the version of) Dora (I will be presenting to Lev) in years. A rare instance of a man touching Martina gently and tenderly. The waiter brings our main meal. A single tear spills from my eye, and lands on the edge of my plate. The plate is full of pasta, with mushrooms and cream. I watch the tear slide into the sauce.

When I look up, his eyes are wet, too.

We agree to talk about nicer things. We talk a little about our jobs – the ups and downs of working for the public sector. I bitch a little about the local party men in a low voice and ask him not to repeat anything. He tells me about the ways the officials interfere with work at the water company – how these little men with their little ideas and little budgets think they can come in and decide what does and doesn't get repaired – who gets water and when for the sake of saving a few pennies here and there.

Then we talk about books – our favourite types of daily broadcasts.

'Oh, did you see last night's?' I ask. 'It was so lovely.' He nods. Both of our faces are pink with the wine we've drunk. He takes my hand again.

'It made me think about you,' he says. 'Sorry. I probably shouldn't have said that – that was—'

I lay my hand over his.

'It made *me* think about *you*.'

He puts his other hand on top of mine, and grins. His teeth are white and crooked. All four of our hands are piled on top of each other in the middle of the table, arms wound around our empty plates. When the waiter comes, we do not let go, make him pry the plates from between our elbows. No dessert. We go for a walk instead. When I stand, I think about how drunk I am, and the fact that I'm not supposed to drink. That if I'm caught drinking, they'll send me to a women's labour camp. He is drunk, too. Both of us are pleasantly drunk. Enough to giggle but not to slur – to stumble, but not to fall.

We agree to walk through the park – I don't mention that walking through the park will take us straight to my apartment. If we fall in love (when we are in love) this will become difficult – lying both deliberately and by omission. But I put that to one side for now, for the sake of tonight. For the sake of a few nights, I hope, before things become strange and complicated.

But as we discover that we have the same favourite flavour of ice cream, and that we love the same books and hate the same music, I wonder if perhaps – he might love me despite everything. That he will dedicate himself to me. That he will come to love Martina as he loves Dora.

In the orange glow of the street lamps, in the moonlight, I have gotten so far ahead of myself. He takes my arm, and I sigh softly.

'I'm so glad you mixed up that meeting,' I say. Lev looks down at me and smiles, eyes crinkling at the corners.

'So am I.'

'My apartment is just over there,' I say, pointing at my building. 'I can lend you that book I was telling you about.'

We do not look at my books.

We go into my apartment and take off our shoes and our coats and I turn to ask him if he'd like anything to drink. But I don't finish my sentence because he has backed me into the wall. Then he is kissing me. His mouth is wet and hot, and tastes of garlic and wine. Martina would wrap her leg around his thighs, pull him in. But I don't think Dora would do that. I moan, softly, as if I'm surprised by all this. I plant one hand in the middle of his back and put the other on the back of his neck, tangling my fingers in his hair.

His mouth leaves mine, and moves across my jaw, down to my neck. His five o'clock shadow is rough, almost like sandpaper – almost painful against the tender skin of my throat. He squeezes one of my breasts, then feels around for a zipper on my dress – finding it, pulling it down and unhooking my brassiere confidently and easily. He leans back, and looks at me, because Dora has gone quiet and still.

'Is this okay?' he asks. 'You can tell me to stop.'

'It's been years since anyone has touched me,' I say. This is not true, not for Dora or Martina. It has been a few months – I last had sex with a strange man I met in a bar I shouldn't have gone to. I suppose it would be true to say it has been years since anyone has touched me with any kindness or affection. Years since anyone who seemed to care about me has touched me. Years since I've been held and caressed and made love to instead of grabbed and poked at and fucked.

'It's been a long time for me, too,' he says. 'I don't usually do this. I feel like a teenager.' He laughs. I move my thigh and realise he's already hard. He hooks his fingers into the collar of my dress and pulls it down. It's loose at the waist and the hips, so it drops, pooling around my ankles, leaving me in my tights and an unhooked bra. Presumptuously, I wore matching underwear. The last man I was with noticed, and said: *So you were expecting to get it tonight, huh?* And he sounded stern – like a woman who'd merely gotten carried away with a man was one he disapproved of less than a woman who went out looking for one.

Matching underwear wasn't very Dora, upon reflection. But it was very Martina.

Usually, Dora doesn't really have sex. Martina does that. Dora goes away for a little while during the act itself because I've never thought about how Dora might fuck. Dora will never see most of these men again. But I like Lev. Lev makes my stomach tight and my thighs warm. So, I have to think about how Dora would do this.

Would Dora tentatively shake off the bra or hug it to her chest. I don't know what to do. The indecision, I realise, is in character. I lean in to that – standing there, looking at Lev, waiting for him to make the next move. He drops to his knees, pulls my tights down to my knees and he looks up at me as he rests his fingertips against the elastic waist-band of my underwear. His eyes look big like this – he looks younger and sweeter. I shudder, but Dora twists her mouth, as if she's unsure – as if no one has ever done this for her. He pulls down my underwear and rests his hands on my hips.

He licks his lips. I tip my head back. Dora is too demure to watch. But Martina sneaks a look after a few minutes – Lev's nose buried in my pubic hair, eyes closed, brow creased with concentration. I stroke his hair, he digs his fingernails into my skin.

I make it to the stage in the dream tonight – but I do not wake when the cage rattles. The emcee is painted like a mime – the only unmasked man in the room. The musicians cease to play.

Mesdames et messieurs . . . S'il vous plaît!

A crowd assembles around me in fine clothes and masks, and lifts me onto the stage, plucking me from my feet and depositing me in the spotlight, working together like one enormous hand.

And now . . . The main event!

The emcee takes my hand – we bow, he crushes my fingers in his grip. An ornate cage lowers from the ceiling, pretty and gold – inside it there is a child. A boy or a girl – I'm not sure. Serene in a thin white gown, it sits on its knees, arms slack by its sides, knuckles on the bottom of the cage, fingers curling upwards into its palms. Its eyes are closed.

It has white skin and white eyelashes. First, I thought its white hair hung down to its shoulders – then I realise it hangs down to the floor of the cage – I had mistaken it for part of the gown. Its teeth and lips are black; its nails and fingertips are black. It opens its eyes, and they are black, too. Hard and shiny, like the eyes you'd find on a toy.

The emcee is still holding my hand. I know he is looking at me. I know he is smiling and that this smile is not a good sign. I know what will come next, and I hope that I will wake up soon. Then I do wake up. In the moments before consciousness, the emcee's smile breaks and he glares at me, as if he knows I wanted to leave, that I am escaping.

I wake with a start in Lev's arms. We are unshowered and tangled in my sheets. We are satisfied and relaxed. His eyes flutter open as I wake.

'I had a nightmare,' I whisper.

'Poor thing,' he says.

He wakes up later than I do, so I jump into the shower, and redo my make-up and hair. I make him a cup of coffee. He startles when I wake him, he refuses my coffee and begins dressing and loudly panicking about the time. He does this even though coffee is expensive, and I made it for him specially. He says he's sorry but he actually has to work today – he meant to get up earlier, he hadn't expected to end up back at my apartment. He dashes out, looking dishevelled and without brushing his teeth.

I drink both cups of coffee and try not to cry. I wash my sheets and shower again, and I scrub off the make-up and the perfume and the last traces of his smell. I cry into a magazine article about keeping a man, and then I cry into a book. And then I slap myself hard on the head over and over again in the hope that this will fix me, and make me normal, and knock all the nasty thoughts from my skull. But it simply makes my head hurt.

I think about Lev's dead son, and the terrible accident. I hope it wasn't a car accident. Thinking about Lev's son, and thinking about car accidents, and with last night's wine drying out my mouth and seeping out of my pores – I end up vomiting. The coffee probably upset my stomach.

I cry into the toilet and I wonder if Lev could tell. If he could smell the reek of Martina beneath Dora's sweet, delicate perfume.

I calm down and eat something, and then I lose it again when I realise how late it is, and that my phone hasn't rung.

No dream for me because I don't sleep.

I look terrible at work the next day, so much so that one of my many bosses calls me *poor lamb* and tells me that I'll find another husband eventually.

I stare at the hallway like Lev might walk into it. I stare at my phone like he might be the one to call it. When it rings, it's just that awful hang-up caller again.

At home, I pace and wait for him to call. I am exhausted. Dora wouldn't fall apart over a man like this – but at home I am just myself, just Martina. And Martina is pacing, frothing, desperate for Lev to call her, to validate the feelings she has for him. If Lev could love Dora, that means he would love Martina, too, and that would be her absolution. I am hysterical. I am thinking about car accidents and Lev and his lost little boy and that, that is when the phone rings.

I take deep breaths and blow the snot from my nose, letting it drip down my face as I dash to the phone. When I speak my voice is thick, but my sinuses sound clear at least.

'Hello, Novak residence?' I say, in a sing-song voice.

'Hi, Dora, it's Lev,' he says. I am euphoric. Tears of relief spill down my cheeks. 'Sorry I had to dash out yesterday morning.'

'Oh, no, don't worry about it. I was busy in the afternoon, you saved me the trouble of throwing you out,' I say. He laughs.

'That's good. I hope you don't mind me calling so soon,' he says.

'No, not at all.'

'I was wondering if you'd be free tomorrow evening, I know it's short notice.'

'Hmm . . .' I say. 'Hang on, let me check my date book.' I hug the phone to my chest, and stand still, staring at my old chintzy furniture and then my old floral carpet. 'Yes, I think that works. Well – it would depend on the time you'd like to meet.'

'What works for you?'

'Um . . . Could you hang on till seven?'

'Of course,' he says.

★

I see Lev almost every night for the next two weeks. It becomes clear to me that this is not the convenient covenant of two people with dead spouses – this is real. I barely think about his dead son, and I even consider warning my father about him. *I've met someone – should I tell him the truth?* And he'll tell me no and tell me to break it off. My papa wants me to remain a spinster as long as I remain Dora.

When we first created Dora, when Papa was in the process of finding me the apartment and the job – he said that I did not deserve happiness. No man deserved to be lumped with me, and a woman who had done the things I had should not be allowed to have a child of her own. I'd be an unfit mother and there's no telling what would happen to it. At the time it was difficult to argue with him – I was still drinking despite the terms of my parole; I had just barely avoided a labour camp thanks to my father's connections.

But I think Dora could have a child. I think Dora could be happy.

Lev is at my apartment one day when my father calls. I have to shush him.

'Hi, Marti,' he says.

'Hello, Papa,' I reply. And he asks me about my week; we do the usual, polite song and dance. On the other end of the phone, I am sure he is assessing me. Do I sound sober? Can he hear anyone in the apartment? Do I sound too happy?

'You missed my call a few days ago, Marti.'

'I was probably at the shop. Maybe the pharmacy.'

'Your appointment is this week, you know,' he says, as if this doesn't happen every month. My regular meeting with a party probation officer is practically synced with my periods. 'You can't miss that.'

'I was just at the store, Papa, I'm sure,' I say. My father grunts down the phone.

When I hang up, Lev asks who I was speaking to. I explain: I have a controlling father, he's very conservative. He doesn't like the idea of me living alone – he thinks I should've moved home as soon as Alexei died. Lev flinches; quite visibly, he flinches.

'Tomas,' he says.

'What?'

'You said Alexei. Your husband's name was Tomas – wasn't it?'

A slip. I blink and shake my head.

'Alexei is my father's name. I dread to think what a therapist would make of that,' I say. I'm still shaking my head. Lev laughs after a moment – an odd pause, as if he forgot how to.

Lev and I go out for dinner. I tell him more made-up stories about Dora's father. I tell Lev that even from a great distance he controls me and makes my life difficult and lonely. I tell Lev that Papa doesn't want me to remarry – that he thinks my marriage to Tomas transcends life and death.

'That's very outdated,' Lev agrees. Still, he is quiet all night. A little distant – so I try harder. I laugh more and bat my eyelashes at him, and I toss my hair and touch his arm. He is colder with me. Not so cold that I could ask him what was wrong – I would look insane. This is behaviour you could attribute to a bad day at work, to a stomach ache, to being a little tired.

In bed things are off, too. I'm on top – I perform for him. I groan and toss my head and touch my breasts. He watches me with forced interest, then he watches the ceiling and then he closes his eyes, squeezing them tight shut. I tell myself that he's just close, that he's about to come – but then he goes a little soft inside of me. He slips out of me, and he's too soft to get it back in.

I tell him it's fine, I already came (I didn't) – then he kisses me and apologises. He tells me he's exhausted and falls asleep. After a while, I fall asleep, too.

I haven't had the dream for a while, but I have it again that night. I seem to fly through the snow – I am immediately escorted to the stage. The dream will not meander tonight – I must face my audience. I must perform.

The emcee opens the cage, then presses a large, curved knife into my palm. He drags the child from the cage and lies it down on the floor. It does not move. It stares blankly up at the ceiling. Its lips part, and it begins to drool. The emcee kisses me on the mouth – he has two tongues.

He turns me around so I am facing the strange, mono-chrome child. He tears my dress open so the audience can see my breasts; he squeezes them, and the crowd cheers. I no longer feel in control of my faculties – so I wave, and I laugh. I hold the knife up, and the emcee kisses my neck, smearing greasepaint on my skin.

He lets go of me, the crowd chants, and I know what I must do. I straddle the child. I raise the knife, I plunge it into the child's chest. I make its white gown a deep, luxurious shade of red.

Then, it sits up and screams. It grabs my face, and opens its mouth, and screams. Then its eyes don't seem as lifeless. Then, I can see the whites of them.

Now we are nearing the end of the dream. The dream always starts the same way, but the ending varies. Sometimes, an orgy around the slaughtered child's corpse. Sometimes, the child pulls its intestines from the cavity of its torso and chokes me with them. Sometimes, the child takes a bite from my cheek. Sometimes, the child takes my breast into its mouth, and drinks my blood while the crowd descends and rips us both apart.

Tonight, I wake up in Lev's arms.

'I had a nightmare,' I whisper. He doesn't say anything.

★

'I always forget what I'm supposed to call you,' the parole officer says.

'Either name is fine,' I assure him.

'How is work?' asks the parole officer. I nod. 'And your identity – that's secure, you think? No trouble?'

'Well . . . There's . . . I've been getting these hang-up calls. For a while,' I say. The parole officer frowns. Asks me if I mean at home or at work. I tell him work, and he relaxes.

'You operate the phone line, yes?'

'Yes, but—'

'Are you sure it's not a problem down your end? Have you had someone check the phone?'

'Not yet,' I say. The parole officer rolls his eyes. He tells me to call the phone company. Then he puts a specimen cup on the table. I don't always have to give them a sample, but I haven't drunk for a week, just in case.

'If you could go and give us your sample,' he says.

I deposit a warm cup of piss at the reception – then I take a bus to work.

It is the day of Lev's meeting, so I am dressed up for him. My colleagues tell me I look nice today. When the time for the meeting with the water company arrives – Lev does not. A woman comes instead, a woman with a hard face in an ugly suit. During the meeting I take minutes. I frown. Perhaps he's sick. Perhaps it was decided this woman should take the meeting instead. It makes me uneasy. When he isn't in the park at lunchtime, I worry.

The phone rings constantly, and when I pick it up there is no answer.

'Who is this?' I hiss. '*Who the fuck is this?*' No answer – the phone hangs up. I slam the handset down against the receiver repeatedly.

'Dora?' the accountant asks. I don't respond to that name. '*Dora.*'

'*What?!*' I snarl. The accountant asks me if it is my time of the month. I tell her it is. Then she calls the phone company for me.

I call Lev at home, but he doesn't answer. He must be sick, I decide. I think about going to his home, and then it occurs to me – I've never been to his apartment. He's mentioned where he lives, but I don't have an address, just a phone number.

I'm supposed to see him tomorrow – he's supposed to come over for dinner. Then he doesn't turn up. *He found out what I did*, is all I can think. *He knows who I am.*

When my father calls that night I ask him: 'Do you have something to do with this?' through tears. 'Did you tell him? Did you make him go away?'

'Him?' he says. He's furious with me. He never shouts – just sighs. 'You're like a man, Marti, that's your problem. You think with what's between your legs and you get stupid. Whoever this man is – if he's gone, if he found out what you did – you did that. I didn't do that. If you don't want things like this to happen – don't see men. Don't sleep around.'

I go to an off-licence, and I buy two bottles of wine, and I begin drinking, staring at the door, periodically calling Lev's house, breathing heavily into the receiver.

Then, a little before midnight – a knock at the door. I run to answer it, skidding on my socks.

It's Lev. His clothes are the same. His face and hair are the same. His demeanour is different. He pushes past me. He ignores me when I cry for him. Where have you been, where were you, why aren't you picking up my calls, what's the matter with you, is something wrong, is everything okay, did I do something wrong. Finally, I ask:

'Do you know? Did you find out?'

He drinks from my wine bottle. He looks at me – no warmth in his eyes. Devoid of affection.

'I always knew, Martina,' he says. 'I took a gamble that you wouldn't recognise me. I didn't think you would; but I worried you might.' He smiles at me. It's a sad smile. All I can do is stand there. I swallow. My stomach, my throat, my intestines all twist into one huge knot inside of me.

Then he gives me his real name. Leon Nebel. Dora doesn't know the name Nebel. Dora doesn't know what any of this is about. Dora is sweet and kind – Dora is devastated. Dora is gone now. Shattered.

'Alexei's father. You used to have a beard,' I say. He tells me not to use his son's name. 'Are you going to kill me?' I ask. He shrugs.

'I was going to. Though I think this life might be punishment enough, in some ways,' he says. He looks around my barren little apartment, where there are no photographs on the walls, and no knick-knacks – no evidence of a life being lived aside from my half-read books, a stack of women's magazines and a few dirty dishes in the sink. A scarf he left here last week, by mistake, is draped over the arm of the sofa because I sniffed it when I felt sad.

'You have no friends. Your family don't want anything to do with you. A few men here and there but . . . no one with any *real* interest in you.' He laughs at me. 'You don't even have any hobbies. You seem to read a little, you watch the daily broadcasts. But that's all I've gathered. Your life is just your sad little job and your nightmares; waiting for some man to come along and save you, love you.'

He'd been watching me for weeks before we met. He didn't lie about the circumstances of his wife's death. She had died of cancer – she had refused treatment, she *had* been a shell of a person since I drunkenly ploughed my father's car into her son. For years Lev, Leon, had stewed over the fact I'd escaped justice – that Papa's party connections had saved me from prison and bought me a new identity.

When his wife died, he felt confident he now had nothing else to live for. He decided to throw his life and too much of his money away in pursuit of finding and killing me. He came to the capital, sought out a private investigator whose fear of party repercussions could be circumvented with enough money. They found me. They followed me. They photographed me. They saw me at work, they saw me with men, they saw me drinking, they saw that I was often alone. Leon stopped paying the private investigator and began to watch me himself. He began to formulate a plan.

He'd seen that I was lonely, and he'd seen that I was desperate, so he invented Lev – the nice man from the water company. He trusted that I'd be too pleased to have Lev's attention to question his presence. He assumed I would not recognise him. He guessed that after so many years I would have let my guard down. He'd seen how poor my judgement was.

'You don't drive, at least. But otherwise . . .' He shakes his head at me. I shrink beneath his gaze. 'The fact you haven't killed yourself is only a testament to your cowardice.'

'So you're going to do it for me?' I ask. And I start to cry, and he doesn't even flinch. 'You might as well get it over and done with.' He takes a step towards me, and I take a step back. We do this until I am backed against the wall. Part of me hopes that he might kiss me. He does not. 'I . . . Can I ask you a question?'

'No,' he says.

'Were you the one calling me?' I ask. He puts his hands around my throat. 'The hang-up caller? The person harassing me at work?' I squeak, before he begins putting pressure on my windpipe.

'I don't know what you're talking about,' he says. He begins squeezing my neck.

And I decide this will be a fitting death for me – strangled to death by my lover. I decide to forget that he was not truly my lover, and that I am the woman who killed his child. In this moment, I think of him only as Lev from the water company. I hold his wrists – at first I stroke them with my thumbs – then I begin to fight back. I fight back when it really starts to hurt, when I feel the pressure building up behind my eyes, when my face begins to feel like it might pop. An instinctual action – because I would be happy to die here. I am happy to be murdered if it means I will not die alone. I hope Lev will kill himself after he kills me. And I hope the police will find us together.

I cannot speak to beg – perhaps this is why he chose to choke me. We are both crying, which moves me.

'Alexei,' he says. 'Alexei.' This is the last thing I hear before I black out.

I wake up again in the snow. On my back and sunk deep into it – usually I am standing. Everything is numb with cold. I struggle to my feet and wade through the snow. I smell the smoke and the animal shit. I reach the tent. I push through the crowd, and they put me on the stage. The emcee lowers the cage.

Tonight, the cage is empty. Tonight, they push me inside. They haul me up to the ceiling, and there I remain. I watch over the crowd; I watch them dance and drink and eat and fuck and dance and drink and eat. I lose track of time. I never sleep but I'm always a little tired. I'm never bored, but I'm never having fun, either. I'm never hungry, but never full. I know I'm waiting for something, but I'm not sure what.

Then I know. One time (it's always the same long, never-ending night, now) I see him. Lev, Leon, wading through the crowd. He looks confused. This is the first time he's made it all the way to the stage.

The musicians cease to play.

Mesdames et messieurs . . . S'il vous plaît!

Content Guide

'Build a Body Like Mine' is about the narrator's long-term issues with disordered eating. It contains detailed discussions of body image, as well as detailed descriptions of binge-eating, purging and restrictive eating. The narrator encourages the reader to follow a destructive method to lose weight. However, no specific weights or body measurements are mentioned.

This story also contains: descriptions of food, parasitic infestations and vomit.

'The Problem Solver' centres on the aftermath of the protagonist's rape by a casual acquaintance. The rape itself is not described in any detail.

This story also contains: references to non-consensual groping and descriptions of violence.

'She's Always Hungry' takes place in a matriarchal village, where men are heavily subject to gendered repression and systemic violence.

This story also contains: descriptions of violence and some body-horror themes.

'The Shadow Over Little Chitaly' contains extensive descriptions of food.

'Hollow Bones' features a protagonist in recovery from a mysterious accident in a science-fiction setting. The story heavily features graphic descriptions of wounds, medical-ised drug use and parasitic infestation.

This story also contains: graphic descriptions of violence and unintentional self-harm.

'Goth GF' contains workplace bullying and references to self-harm.

'Extinction Event' centres on the discovery of a new plant-like species that may help humanity avoid a climate apoc-alypse. Climate change is the core theme of the story. While human characters in the story are not subject to violence, the new species featured in the story undergo disturbing transformations – including developing pustules and rot – which are described in detail.

'Nightstalkers' is set in the 1970s and contains period-typical homophobia as well as recreational drug use.

'Shake Well' is a story about a black-market cure for acne.

The story heavily features a relationship between a teen-aged protagonist and her abusive older boyfriend – alluding frequently to grooming and sexual violence.

The story also contains: graphic descriptions of recreational drug use, acne, popping pimples, picking skin, scabs and other body-horror themes centring on skin.

'The King' contains graphic descriptions of violence and cannibalism, as well as references to racism, sexual violence and apocalyptic themes.

'Company Man' contains graphic descriptions of violence, references to alcoholism, and centres on a relationship that could be viewed as non-consensual in retrospect.

Acknowledgements

I'd like to thank my partner George, my parents and friends and to once again extend my eternal gratitude to New Writing North. The oldest stories in this collection date back to 2018 and were written while I was on the Young Writers Talent Fund under the tutelage of the great writer Matt Wesolowski, who I would also like to give special thanks.

Thank you to my agents Rachel Mann and Marc Simonsson and the team at Faber (particularly Libby Marshall, Sara Helen Binney and Hannah Turner) for their continued support.

I would also like to thank Clare Bogen at 3 of Cups Press who published an early version of 'Build a Body Like Mine', and the staff at *Granta* magazine who featured the title story 'She's Always Hungry' in the Best of Young British Novelists 2023 issue.

And, as always, to my readers. Your continued enthusiasm for my work means the world to me.